Breathless, she … the truck. "I need water."

He couldn't help but smile. "Well, you *have* been running." He cringed. Why did he always have to make a dumb joke when he wanted to impress a girl?

She put a hand out to stop herself from slamming right into the truck door. "You said something about mountain spring water in a well. Can you take me to it?"

So that was all she wanted. An irrational disappointment pushed aside his smile. "Sure. Climb in."

As she crossed around to the passenger side, he reached over to open the door, his heart pounding out a stampede.

She jumped in and arranged the bottles on her lap before fastening the seat belt. "Can we hurry? I have to get back to the set."

"No problem." He pulled away from the curb, trying not to glance at her. She was cute, that was for sure, with an intensity he found captivating. He loosened his grip on the wheel. Best to get over this feeling he had about her as quickly as possible.

Or was it?

LESLEY ANN McDANIEL

Though she's a Montana girl at heart, Lesley Ann McDaniel now resides in the Seattle area. She juggles a career in theatrical costuming with writing women's and young adult fiction, along with homeschooling her two daughters. In her spare time she chips away at her goal of reading every book ever written.

LESLEY ANN McDANIEL

Lights, Cowboy, Action

HEARTSONG
· P R E S E N T S ·

Recycling programs for this product may not exist in your area.

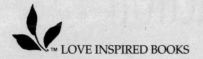

™ LOVE INSPIRED BOOKS

ISBN-13: 978-0-373-48663-2

LIGHTS, COWBOY, ACTION

Copyright © 2013 by Lesley Ann McDaniel

www.LoveInspiredBooks.com

Printed in U.S.A.

Jesus answered, "Everyone who drinks this water will be thirsty again, but whoever drinks the water I give them will never thirst. Indeed, the water I give them will become in them a spring of water welling up to eternal life."
—*John* 4:13, 14

This book is dedicated to Jasmine, Olivia and Brent,
who tolerate sharing a house with a writer.
Also, to my critique partner, Lynnette,
and the rest of my amazing critique group.
Without them, I'd never make it past the rough draft.

Chapter 1

Courtney Jacobs doubted there could be enough coffee in all of Thornton Springs, Montana, to see her through this movie shoot.

After filling her paper cup with the morale-boosting brew, she headed back toward the set. All around her, sleep-deprived crew members hustled to transform this charming burg into an old Western town. She checked her watch. 7:00 a.m. Within an hour, Keith Kingsley, the temperamental director of *North to Montana*—*N2M* to insiders—would be ready to call "action," and he wasn't exactly known for his patience.

"Move it or bleed!" A rigger bellowed as he charged past, swinging an aluminum grip stand just over Courtney's head.

She danced around a coil of electrical cables then side-stepped a set painter as he examined the distressing he'd given a storefront. Wincing as the gaffer shouted out coarse instructions to his crew of lighting techs, she ducked to avoid a swooping boom pole.

A contented sigh slipped through her lips. With just four independent films on her résumé—two a year since graduating from college—she felt lucky to have booked a major studio-backed project so early in her career.

She'd been hired as personal assistant to the star, Angela Bijou—an A-list actress with a reputation for supreme diva behavior and for taking up with her leading men. Angela had made it clear from day one that Jeffrey Mark Caulfield (sizzling from the recent success of *The Pharaoh's Tomb*), would be no exception.

The *bleep* of Courtney's cell phone drew her from her wandering thoughts. Balancing her still-full cup on the edge of her clipboard, she opened a text from the key costumer.

Ms. Bju s neded 4 a finl fttng of hr Act 3 pRT gwn 2moro @ 2. B sur sh's thr.

Courtney gnawed at her lower lip. If *Ms. Bijou* didn't know about the *fttng,* it would be one more thing for her to take out on Courtney.

Hurrying down the center of the newly dirt-encrusted street, she clenched her cup between her teeth and shoved her clipboard under her arm. She flicked open the phone keyboard and tapped out a response while dodging a gaggle of grips positioning an old wooden wagon by the edge of the just-built boardwalk.

2moro @ 2. No woriez.

Nearing the area where the first scene of the day would be shot, Courtney hit Send and scanned the street. Several cast members milled about in costume but—no surprise—Angela wasn't among them. Giving a cursory glance to the berry-pink Swatch she'd been given as a thank-you from her actress on her last movie, she headed toward the makeup trailer in the hope that Angela had made it to her call on time.

Striding across the set, she drank in the liveliness of her surroundings. It was great being a part of something this vital. So what if her job at the moment was keeping the leading lady on-schedule? She was an indispensable cog in the machine.

"Court-*neeey!*"

Stopping in her tracks, Courtney spun around to face the familiar angry command. From the first day of rehearsals, Angela Bijou had demonstrated an annoying articulation of Courtney's name that made the word itself sound like an outright accusation.

"You had better explain what's going on here!" The woman stormed toward Courtney with a heated, resolute gait and fire in her famous jade-green eyes. Her flimsy peach-silk coverup and matching turban signified that she hadn't yet made it to hair or wardrobe, and screamed "Look at me—I'm a star."

Courtney opened her mouth to respond, but Angela cut her off with a tirade that rivaled a hurricane.

"Are you completely incompetent?" Angela screeched as she planted her lithe form two feet from where Courtney stood.

As the blood rose to her face, Courtney became painfully aware that the entire cast and crew had turned to gawk. "What's the matter, Ms. Bijou?" She fought to keep her tone level.

"What's the matter?" Angela tossed her platinum pincurled head back with such force her tiny neck made a faint cracking sound. "The 'matter' is that I have no water in my trailer."

Courtney let that register. All this fuss over a plumbing problem?

"D'eau Douce." Angela crossed her willowy arms. "Imported from France. Does that ring a bell? I'm supposed to

have four sixteen-ounce bottles chilling in my trailer every morning when I arrive."

"Oh…" Courtney skimmed her memory. "For…drinking?"

"Yes, for *drinking*." Angela gave her a scowl that implied she should audition for the next season of *American Idiot*. "I wash my face in pure Norwegian spring water, which by the way I didn't see in there, either."

Courtney heard herself utter something about making a few phone calls to Norway as she took a giant step backward.

"Look." Angela apparently wasn't done yelling. "I need sixty-four ounces a day. How else am I supposed to keep my skin so youthful and clear?" She drew her fingertips across her youthful, clear cheek for emphasis. "Every. Single. Day."

"Uh…okay, Ms. Bijou." Courtney scribbled out a note on the top page of her clipboard as she took a half step in what she hoped was the direction of water of all desirable nationalities. A thought stopped her cold. "Was that sixty-four ounces of the drinking water or the washing kind?"

Angela's eyes narrowed. "Don't play dumb. Obviously, you *knew* about this."

Gripping her half cup of tepid coffee between her thumb and her index finger, Courtney flipped through the papers on her clipboard as if to exonerate herself from this allegation. She knew nothing about her actress's water preference and made a mental note to be sure always to ask in the future.

With what she hoped would read as a competent smile, she turned to go, smacking into a carpenter as he flew past with an armload of railroad ties. Coffee flew from her cup, splashing across her papers and down the front of her sea-green T-shirt. She winced.

Angela's shrieking voice rang out from behind. "Check my contract! I need my water every day I'm on the set. I'm supposed to have it!"

Courtney clutched her clipboard to her stained front and darted toward what appeared to be a grocery store on the next block. If the past five minutes were any indication of things to come, this shoot was going to be a nightmare.

"Yes, sir, this is just about the biggest thing that's ever happened in this town." Cal wiped his hands on his apron and stretched a long gaze out the front window of his general store.

Casting a dubious glance at Cal from under the brim of his Stetson, Adam Greene drew in a long breath. It was great that the movie people were boosting the town's flagging economy, but apart from that he really didn't see what all the fuss was about. "Say, Cal, you got any of those red lentils left? Janessa made a killer stew last week and I'd like her to surprise us with a repeat performance."

Cal wrested his attention away from the window. "That sister 'a yours is gettin' to be more like your mama every day. A regular Mary Stewart."

Adam grinned. "I think you mean Martha. Martha Stewart. Don't tell Janessa that, though. She's dead set against the idea of making some lucky man a great wife someday."

Cal's head bobbed as he grabbed a jar of beans off a shelf. "Still determined to get outta Dodge now that she's graduated high school, eh?"

"She's got plans." Adam studied a barrel of apples. "Nothing wrong with that."

"Not a thing. I just know you and your mama will miss her is all."

"True." Grabbing the brown bag of lentils Cal had filled for him, Adam raised an earnest smile. He had a full seven years on his baby sister and had been the man of the house since their father's death when Adam was fifteen. It was strange to think of her leaving the nest. "Far be it from me to stand in the way of an ambitious female—"

Abruptly, the front door burst open and in flew a young woman gripping a clipboard and a paper coffee cup. She pushed a strand of sandy-blond hair from her forehead with the rim of the cup as she scanned the store, urgency fairly sparking from her hazel eyes. Adam's gaze dawdled a little longer than he liked to consider gentlemanly.

As she surged purposefully toward the counter, his eyes followed. She looked young and pretty in a fresh-faced, no makeup sort of way. Judging from the walkie-talkie clipped to her belt, she must be some sort of behind-the-scenes worker, not an actress. A corner of his mouth lifted. Maybe having the movie people in town wouldn't be such a bad thing after all.

Cal lit up. "What can I do for you, young lady?"

She spoke with a resolute clip. "Please tell me you carry *D'eau Douce*."

The smile slid from Cal's face. "Doe Do... What?"

"It's French." She tapped the clipboard with the cup and scouted around some more.

Sensing that Cal could use a hand on this one, Adam stepped up to the counter. "Excuse me, ma'am. Maybe I can help...uh...*translate?*"

"Sure." Avoiding his gaze, she continued to search the shelves. "Do you speak 'actress'?"

"I'm sorry, no." While he felt for her obvious United Nations dilemma, he couldn't help but dwell on how pretty she was. "What exactly is this thing you're looking for?"

"Water." She moved a few feet to peruse the refrigerator case where Cal kept the milk and juice. "What kind of mineral water do you carry?"

Adam cast an amused glance at Cal, whose expression had grown even more befuddled.

"I don't— I mean—" Cal stammered.

Seeing where this was going, Adam chimed in. "You'll be hard-pressed to find any of those fancy bottled waters here, ma'am."

As her head snapped toward him, their eyes met for the first time. "No water? But what do people here drink?"

Adam tipped a shrug. "We drink well water, mostly. We've got the best mountain spring water you've ever tasted. I'd be happy to—"

"No. I mean… Thank you." Shifting the cup to the hand that held the clipboard, she pulled a cell phone out of a pouch on her waistband, and started punching in numbers as she moved toward the door. Looking back, her eyes rested briefly on Adam. "Thanks, anyway." With a slight smile, she yanked open the door and bolted out.

Leaning against the counter, Adam pushed his hat back a touch and folded his arms.

Cal gave him a good-natured cuff to the bicep. "Shouldn't you be finishing that shopping?"

"Shopping?" Adam nodded slowly. "Oh. Right."

Courtney surveyed the street as she darted toward the set, her hope of finding a specialty food store growing dimmer by the second. Her mind whirred. The only thing she could think of was to call the safe, actress-free office of her BFF back in L.A.

"Sheila Macintosh here."

Courtney breathed out relief at the familiar greeting. "Thank *goodness* you're there."

"Hey, Court." Sheila let out a little titter. "Don't tell me you're homesick already."

"Not unless by 'homesick' you mean 'desperately missing the Von's delivery boy.'" Courtney firmed her resolve. "Sheil, I need you to do me a huge favor."

"Is it a favor for you or for Angela Bijou, 'cause you know I don't cater to queen bees."

"Consider it a favor to your best friend who wants to stay employed. I need you to source some bottled water for me. I'll give you all my info so you can order it and have it billed to the movie."

"They don't have water in Montana?" Sheila quipped. "How do they get the mountains so green?"

"Funny. Of course they have water, just not the right kind." Courtney stopped walking, not wanting anyone of importance to overhear her plight. "Will you do it?"

"I'm ready to write." Sheila's tone warmed. "Just remember, you owe me a dinner at Mr. Chow when you get back."

"On *my* salary? Better make it Del Taco." Courtney rattled off the details of Angela's demand, hoping this wouldn't be the first of many. "Tell them I need it ASAP. Hire a private jet if you need to."

Sheila grunted. "Movie people are weird."

"You said it." She started walking again.

"Before you go…" Sheila's voice grew coy. "You have to tell me. Is Jeffrey Mark Caulfield as hot in a cowboy hat as he is in a pith helmet?"

"I haven't seen him in costume yet." Courtney's mind wandered back to the store she'd left a few minutes before—to that tall, handsome hottie in the dusty blue jeans and well-worn boots. "He's got nothing on the *real* cowboys out here, though."

"Oh, really?" Sheila crooned. "Any one in particular?"

"Well…" Courtney's face flushed. What was she doing? She had far too much to deal with to let herself get distracted by an admittedly attractive guy. Especially one she most likely wouldn't even run into again. Still, she couldn't lie, especially to Sheila. "Okay, yes. One that I just met was… movie-star handsome. And nice, too. Really nice."

"Uh-huh. So they grow 'em handsome out there. Must be in the water."

Courtney smiled. "Yeah, it's the mountain spring water."

"So, you *will* be coming home when this movie is finished shooting, right? Or will you be changing your name to Mrs. Handsome Cowboy and learning to rope cattle?"

Courtney sneered at the phone. "Oh, you are so very funny.

Just get my water ordered and pray I still have my job by the time it gets here."

"Sure thing. Oh, and that's not the only thing I'll be praying for, Mrs. Handsome Cowboy."

Clicking her cell phone off, Courtney took a deep breath. Sure that guy seemed really great but this was the last thing she needed. She was here to do a job, not fall for some guy who lived a world away from everything important to her. Letting herself get caught up in thinking about him would just be irresponsible.

Her pace slowed as she neared the set. Why did Angela's personal drought suddenly not feel quite so urgent? Thinking about the cowboy seemed to have a mysteriously calming effect on her. She shook it off. With a major problem to solve, she had too much on her mind to leave her head in the clouds.

Chapter 2

As he loaded his groceries into the back of his pickup, Adam couldn't help but take a look down the street at the movie hullabaloo. What was all that fuss about, anyway? Of course, the financial shot in the arm had been an answer to prayer, no denying that. He shrugged. It would all be over soon enough.

Tossing the last box into the back of the truck, his eye hooked on the attractive young woman with the water quandary standing in the middle of the next block talking animatedly into her phone. Hopefully, the person on the other end was more helpful than he'd been. He mentally kicked himself. Why had he offered her well water? He must have sounded like a real hayseed.

And why couldn't he take his eyes off her? Sure, she had turned his head like no one in this town had managed to do in a very long time, but so what? A woman like her wouldn't look twice at a guy like him, and what could come of it anyway? She wasn't from here, and he had to be careful when it came to matters of the heart.

He forced his attention away from her. One thing he was sure of, it would take a herd of wild horses to drag him away from Thornton Springs. Of course, that did narrow down his choice of women just a bit. While he had never considered himself to be a romantic, he still held out a hope that there was someone special out there for him.

He looked up as she clicked her phone off and started walking. Funny, he didn't even know her name, but she had a magnetic draw on him. He glanced skyward. *Lord, I know You have a plan for my life. If You want me to stay single, please remove this desire for a companion.*

In spite of his best efforts, his focus landed on her one more time. Since her pace had slowed, he figured she must have solved her problem.

On the other hand, Lord—he folded his arms and leaned against the truck—*if You intend for me to find the right woman to marry, please make sure I know her when I see her.*

Allowing that thought to quietly pass, he tried to recall what else he had intended to do in town today. *Feed store... right.* He made his way around the back of the truck. *After that, I could sure use a cup of coffee.*

Courtney lifted her hand to Angela's trailer door, but stopped cold at the sound of an angry male voice.

"Do you really think I'm that dense, Angela?"

Courtney skittered down off the platform. The last thing she wanted was to walk into the middle of a fight between Angela Bijou and Jeffrey Mark Caulfield.

What could she do? Angela was needed on the set soon, and it was Courtney's responsibility to make sure she made it on time. If she breezed into the trailer with an air of authoritative efficiency, it might send the message that their lovers' quarrel would have to wait. On the other hand, the interruption might signify that Courtney thought of herself as more than just an underling, and could easily get her fired. She sighed. Talk about a no-win.

Just as she was about to phone Sheila again and ask what *she'd* do, the door to the trailer burst open and Jeffrey Mark Caulfield, clad in cowboy regalia, stormed down the steps. He spun around and waved a hand in what appeared to be a well-choreographed gesture of intimidation.

"You're unbelievable, Angela!"

Ignoring Courtney, he stomped off toward the set as Angela appeared in the doorway. Courtney breathed out relief at the sight of her in full makeup, wig, and costume. At least she'd had the forethought to fully prepare for the day's shoot before alienating her costar.

"*I'm* unbelievable?" she shrieked. "You're the one who needs to be knocked off your high horse, Mr. Hotshot. Oh, I forgot—you use a stunt double for your riding scenes. My mistake."

She whirled around and disappeared into the trailer, allowing the door to bang shut behind her.

Taking a fortifying breath, Courtney climbed the steps and pushed open the door to find Angela throwing things around the small living room area, muttering to herself.

"Uh…Ms. Bijou?"

"Who does he think he is, anyway?" Angela clearly addressed Courtney now, judging from her increase in volume. "He seems to have forgotten that awful TV series he started out on. And his first movie? Straight to DVD. He thinks *he's* the name on this film? It's like he has no clue what my Q rating is. I've worked hard to get where I am. Doesn't he know that?"

Since she appeared to be awaiting an answer, Courtney responded. "Uh…I'm sure he's aware."

Angela twisted her mouth. "Mmm." Seeming to calm down some, she turned to the lighted mirror on one end of the room and primped her auburn wig. "Where's my water?"

Courtney's throat tightened. This wasn't the best time to break anything less than stellar news. There had to be a way to put a positive spin on her answer. "Well, starting tomorrow you'll have as much *D'eau Douce* as you can drink."

Angela's eyes fired arrows at Courtney's image in the mirror. "Did you say 'tomorrow'? What do you expect me to do *today?*"

Since she hadn't actually worked out the answer to that yet, Courtney could only gulp.

Angela shot across the room and reached into a blue bin with a recycling logo on the side. "Do you see this?" She held up a small, ornately shaped glass bottle with a gold-and-pink fleur-de-lis painted on it. "I brought some with me this morning. Naturally assuming there would be more coming, I used what I had to fill my humidifier." She pitched the bottle at Courtney's feet. "Unless you want to be on the next plane to L.A. begging for your job back at Betty's Big Burger, I'd suggest you get my water here today!"

She charged past Courtney, slamming the door again on her way out. Courtney fought back tears. Did the woman think she had actually worked at Betty's Big Burger or was that just a euphemism?

Bending down, she picked up the empty bottle and tapped it against the edge of her clipboard. She sighed. If only the stupid thing could automatically refill. If only she could track down enough bottles just to get her through the day. Her eyes rested on the blue bin. If only....

Inspiration pinged. She hurried across the room, grateful for Angela being hip to the movie-stars-going-green trend. Kneeling down, she took heart. Three other empties, complete with caps, reclined in the corner of the bin. She lifted them out and hugged all four between her abdomen and the clipboard.

She knew exactly what she needed to do. Next step, track down that handsome and oh-so-helpful cowboy.

Chapter 3

After telling the production assistant she had to run a quick errand for Ms. Bijou, Courtney took off down the street, clutching her precious water bottles and her clipboard. In a town so tiny, that cowboy couldn't have gone far. Her only hope was that he hadn't hopped onto his horse and ridden off into the proverbial sunset. Or sunrise, as the case may be.

As she darted past what looked like a diner, her optimism rose. Inside, a row of Stetson-wearing men edged the counter. With a lineup like that, chances were good that one of them would be her fella.

The smell of bacon and strong coffee welcomed her as she charged through the door and halted at the end of the counter. She let out a huff. As cowboys went, this crowd was more Hoss Cartwright than Texas Ranger.

She made a frenetic visual inspection of the packed café, but none of the faces glancing up at her seemed familiar.

"Help ya, miss?"

She turned as a man approached her behind the counter. A

grease-stained apron covered an equally grimy white T-shirt, but he had a cheerful countenance.

"I hope so," she said. "I'm looking for a cowboy."

In unison, every man seated at the counter glanced up from his breakfast, their forks hovering in midair.

"—I mean," she continued rapidly, "I met a particular cowboy this morning and now I need to ask him a favor."

"I see." The man set down his coffeepot. "Any idea of his name?"

She bit her lip. Precious moments ticked past. "I didn't catch it, but he was tall and dark... Think Hugh Jackman only better."

A murmur went down the row of men, and Courtney scolded herself. Why had she described him in such a giddy, college-girl sort of way?

The man in the apron creased his brow. "Hugh *who?*"

"Uh...Jackman. You know, handsome movie actor...?"

He shook his head, bell apparently unrung.

"Really buff and...um..." Why on earth was she still talking?

The man looked contemplative. "My guess is you mean Adam Greene. That sound right?"

Uh...maybe." Her shoulders tensed. "Have you seen this Adam Greene recently?"

One of the men seated down the row spoke up. "I saw him down at the general store not long ago."

Her heart lifted. "You mean the grocery store?" That would make sense since she'd seen him there herself.

The men all nodded.

"Thanks a lot." Courtney hurried off, hopeful that Adam Greene, if that was her man, was a really slow shopper.

Hurrying back into the same store she'd visited not a half hour before, she scanned the place. It had grown a little busier, but the customers all appeared to be moms with small kids in tow. The storekeeper seemed surprised to see her again.

"Excuse me, sir," she said. "That man who was in here earlier…the one who tried to help me…."

"Oh, you mean Adam."

"Adam. Right." She smiled at the confirmation. "Do you know where he went?"

He stopped to consider. "Let's see. He did say something about heading over to the feed store." His head bobbed toward the front window.

"The feed store? Thanks a lot." Scurrying outside again, she looked straight ahead, relieved to see a large sign that read Duke's Feed, Saddles and More. Giving a cursory glance both ways for traffic, she hurried across the street, hoping her plan would work.

Either that—she reached for the door handle—*or pray that Betty's Big Burger back home is hiring.*

The rich smell of coffee warmed and heartened Adam as he entered Joe's Diner. It had been a busy morning, and he could do with a little kick of caffeine.

"Mornin', Adam." Joe approached with a pot of the warm brew. "What'll it be, son?"

Adam dipped a greeting to Joe's usual morning gang as he took the end counter seat. "Make it a coffee to go, Joe. I've been lollygaggin' too much this morning and I need to get back to the ranch."

"No wonder, what with all the excitement goin' on out there." Reaching behind him, Joe grabbed a tall paper cup and started to pour. "That movie has everyone all worked up."

Adam raised a brow. "Yep, it's pretty much all anybody wants to talk about."

Joe lidded the cup and set it down in front of Adam. "Speakin' o' that, a young lady was just in here askin' after you. I assumed she was from the movie."

"Oh?" He angled a warning at the sideways glances his counter mates offered. "What did she look like?"

"Young. Real pretty. Held on to a clipboard like her life counted on it."

"Oh, really?" A smile curved Adam's lips. "What'd she have to say?"

"Not much. Just lookin' for you. Somethin' to do with usin' the ranch, maybe?"

"I expect so." Standing, Adam picked up his cup and tossed a couple of bills down on the counter. "See ya, Joe."

As he stepped out into the cool morning, Adam took a long swig of coffee and a long look up the street. She'd been asking after him. *Why on earth?*

He shrugged and headed toward his truck. He didn't want to get his hopes up, and besides, if she really wanted to talk to him, he was pretty sure she'd be resourceful enough to track him down.

He wasn't all that hard to find.

If Courtney had ever stopped to picture what the inside of a feed store looked like, this would have been dead on. Dark wood planks creaked as she treaded through the door and inhaled a pungent odor that reminded her of Goldie, the hamster she'd owned as a kid. It wasn't a *bad* smell, just… prominent. The extra-high shelves were crammed with bags of various sizes and colors. Several customers in overalls and ragged jeans milled about with an enthusiasm that people in L.A. only conjured up when shopping for jewelry or shoes. She definitely didn't get small-town priorities.

A man in grubby overalls and a blue work shirt approached her with a warm expression.

"What can I do for ya, Miss?"

"I'm looking for someone named Adam Greene. Do you know him?"

Hooking his fingers in the bib of his overalls, the man grinned. "Since he was barely old enough to help his dad feed the horses. Why, I remember—"

"Have you seen him today?"

His face fell slightly at her lack of interest in his story. "He was in here not ten minutes ago. You just missed him."

Just missed him? She needed water and it had to be tasty enough to fool Angela's discerning palate. Her job and probably her entire career depended on it. "Where did he go?" She stepped closer, tasting the dust from the feed bags he'd probably been hoisting. "Does he have a cell phone or a pager or something?"

"Well…*no*. Not that I know of." His eyes lit on something behind her. "But he does have an old green pickup and he's getting into it right now."

Courtney whirled around and strained to see out the smudgy window. Sure enough, there was her cowboy holding a cup of coffee and getting into the cab of a dirty old truck. She yelped. She had to rope him in before he got away.

Chapter 4

Settling into the driver's seat, Adam took a sip of the just-strong-enough coffee and set the cup in the holder on the dash. Joe's words still gnawed at him. If it hadn't been for the peanut gallery pretending not to be listening in, Adam would have asked more questions. Was this really just about the movie?

He shook off the thought. Even though a small part of him wanted it to be an inquiry of a personal nature, that could only lead to problems. Best not to get anything started. He turned the key in the ignition. Why was he even thinking she might be interested in him? It was probably nothing at all like that. As he checked his side mirror, he suddenly felt a little foolish for even letting the thought cross his mind.

"Adam!"

His head wrenched up and he caught his breath. There she was, the woman who had occupied his thoughts all morning, darting across the street waving an arm and shouting his name.

Nerves racing, he shifted back into Park and rolled down his window.

Breathless, she called out as she neared the truck. "I need water!"

He couldn't help but smile. "Well, you *have* been running." He cringed. Why did he always have to make a dumb joke when he wanted to impress a girl?

She put a hand out to stop herself from slamming right into the truck door. "You said something about mountain spring water in a well. Can you take me to it?"

So that was all she wanted. An irrational disappointment pushed aside his smile. "Sure. Climb in."

As she crossed around to the passenger's side, he reached over to open the door, his heart pounding out a stampede.

She jumped in and arranged the bottles on her lap before fastening the seat belt. "Can we hurry? I have to get back to the set."

"No problem." He pulled away from the curb, trying not to glance at her. She was cute, that was for sure, with an intensity he found captivating. He loosened his grip on the wheel. Best to get over this feeling he had about her as quickly as possible.

Or was it?

Courtney let out a long breath as she settled into the tattered seat of the old truck. A glance at her watch told her that fifteen minutes had already passed since she'd left the set. If Angela needed her and she wasn't at her beck and call, all this effort might be wasted. She swallowed so hard it almost hurt.

As Adam veered the truck off the main street, Courtney clutched the bottles to keep them from rolling off her lap. Looking down, she gasped. She'd all but forgotten about the coffee stain on her shirt, which had been the least of her worries when it had happened. Now, it only added to the less-than-ideal first impression she had no doubt made on this total heartthrob she'd practically kidnapped. He probably thought she was insane. Butterflies filled her stomach and she felt unsure of her next breath.

"So…this is just a wild guess." He slid her an amused look. "You're working on the movie?"

"Oh…yes…" Her heart drummed out an unusual rhythm. "I'm sorry. I don't normally hijack people like this."

A smile dimpled his cheek. "Well, we generally don't mind helping out strangers around here, miss…"

"Oh…*and* I'm normally not so rude." Drawing the clipboard up to conceal the stain, she twisted slightly toward him. "I'm Courtney Jacobs."

He tipped the brim of his cowboy hat with one hand. "It's a pleasure, Miss Jacobs. My name's Adam, but I guess you knew that."

"Yes." A blush crawled up her cheeks. "I hope that wasn't too weird—me hunting you down and all."

"Weird? No. *Unusual,* maybe."

That it was. Why hadn't she explained herself? A sputter erupted where words should have been. "S-see, I'm the personal assistant to Angela Bijou. You know who she is?"

He nodded. "I've seen one or two of her movies."

Of course. This was Montana, not another planet. "So, she sprang this demand for French mineral water on me. I can't get the real stuff till tomorrow, and I'm counting on your well water to fool her."

"Fool her?" A corner of his mouth lifted.

"She doesn't seem to understand that I can't make it to France and back on my coffee break." She blushed, lowering her shield. "I can't even drink my *coffee* on my coffee break." She glanced down at her stained T-shirt. "I tried applying it topically, but it's not the same."

A laugh twinkled in his chocolate-brown eyes. "So, Angela Bijou expects a lot."

She pointed her index finger at him, bingo-style. "That would be an understatement."

He seemed to consider his words. "And you...*like* this job?"

She shot him a look. "I *love* my job." Defensiveness gurgled in her throat. "I'm sure she'll chill out. It's my responsibility to think about what she needs every minute. It's what I was hired to do."

His chin dipped in understanding if not approval. "I see."

Uneasy now at the thought that she might really be in over her head, she turned to peer out the window. She was good at her job, for heaven's sake. Why would she allow self-doubt to creep in?

She feigned interest in the passing scenery. Except for the two-lane highway ribboning between pine-forested mountains, all signs of civilization had been left behind at the outskirts of town. Courtney absentmindedly tapped a bottle against her leg in time with the radio, marveling at the symmetry between the natural beauty around them and Adam's seemingly arbitrary soundtrack. The song modulated up a key just as an impossibly green pasture appeared from around a bend. Beyond it, glorious deep blue mountains appeared matte-painting perfect against the clear morning sky.

Awe surged through her. "This place is amazing." Her insides fluttered as she struggled to find small talk. "So, have you always lived here?"

"All my life." He tilted a nod. "In fact, my great-great-granddad was one of the founding fathers of Thornton Springs. It was a mining boomtown back in the late 1800s."

"Cool." That *was* cool. She envied him having that kind of connection to a place, especially one so idyllic.

"And you?" He sounded so much more at ease than she felt. "Where are you from?"

"Fresno." She relaxed a little, encouraged by his show of interest. "I moved to L.A. after college. Ever been there?"

He shook his head. "Never been much for cities."

"Really? But L.A. has everything...theaters, museums, beaches. Things you don't find in a small town."

"Hey." His tone became playfully defensive. "We've got a playhouse in Helena. Museums, too. As for the beach, we generally make it to Flathead Lake at least once a summer."

She couldn't help but study his features as he spoke. He seemed like the guy who would be cast in the role of handsome Montana cowboy, only he was the real thing. She smiled. "Ok, I was wrong. Smalltownsville has everything we have back home."

He tossed her a glance and a grin. "No, you've got one thing we don't. You can keep your smog. Give me the fresh Montana air any day."

A deep breath quelled her protest. She hadn't really given it much thought, but she'd been breathing easier since she'd gotten here. There was something to be said for that. "But, seriously—" she pivoted her body toward him "—what do you do for fun? I mean, in L.A. you can go to a movie any time of the day. You can shop. Plus we have a million great restaurants."

"Really? A million?" His eyes twinkled. "How many have *you* been to?"

"Well..." She dipped her chin. "A few short of a million. But it's good to know they're there."

"We have restaurants here, too." He tilted his head in her direction while keeping his eyes on the road. "There's the diner, and Guido and Sal's pizza place. For special occasions we go to Esther's Kitchen up in Halston. My sister Janessa works there. Great food. You should try it."

"I'll keep that in mind if I have a special occasion."

An elaborate gate at the start of a long private road off the driver's side of the highway snagged her attention. Two huge wagon wheels bookended mammoth wrought-iron letters that curved across the top, spelling out Bar-G Ranch.

Courtney's eyes widened in recognition. "Hey, that's one

of our locations. We're shooting there for the next couple of weeks."

"I know." Adam nodded toward the gate as they drove past. "In fact, I'll be working around your schedule, trying to keep the animals calm."

"Oh, that's where you work?" She swiveled around to scan the expanse of pasture beyond the gate.

"Yep. As a matter of fact, I—"

"How far is this well, anyway?" She snapped her attention forward, and her neck muscles tensed. This was taking way too long.

"It's just right here." He eased the truck off to the side of the road into a small dirt parking area.

A simple wooden roof on four corner poles covered a couple of metal spouts. Courtney wasn't sure what she'd expected, but this sure wasn't it.

She eyed the spouts suspiciously. "You're sure this water is safe?"

"Believe me, it's all we drink at our place. All most of the town drinks. It tastes better than anything out of a bottle and it's free."

"Free. Great. That ought to offset the cost of the stuff I'm having jetted in from France."

A smirk playing on his lips, Adam opened his door, then reached over to take two of the bottles. "Movie people are something else."

She couldn't help but meet his smile. "You said it."

Chapter 5

By the time they got back to town, Adam had convinced himself that Courtney's interest in him was strictly limited to his ability to help with the water. It was all for the best, although he couldn't deny his disappointment. Not only was she easy on the eyes, she was funny and interesting, and had a way about her that made him long to get to know her better.

"The school is our base camp," she explained as a man waved him into the parking lot of the grade school a block off the main street of town. "You'll have to park over there. They won't risk the sound of cars now that they've started shooting for the day."

Adam obliged, then nodded toward the bottles in her hands. "Let me help you carry those."

"Oh, I can manage." She cradled the bottles in the crook of one arm and opened the passenger's door. "Thanks again. I guess I'll see you—"

"Courtney! Where have you been?" A woman wearing a

headset and a deep frown raced toward them. "Ms. Bijou has been shouting for you. Didn't you get my text?"

"Oh...." The fear in Courtney's lovely eyes melted into decisiveness. She faced Adam. "Would you mind doing me just one more quick favor?" She pointed to a row of Winnebagos that lined one edge of the parking lot. "See that dressing room trailer on the end? The silver-and-pink one? Would you mind running these bottles over there and sticking them in the fridge?"

"Okay, but—"

"Thanks. I owe you one!" She deposited the bottles in his arms, jumped out of the truck and took off with the uptight headset woman.

I owe you one. He chuckled, pleased with her implication that they'd be seeing more of each other.

He got out of the truck, walked to the trailer and tapped lightly on the door. When no one answered, he stepped inside and looked around. A nice-sized living room had a makeup counter on one end and a small kitchen on the other. He crossed over to leave the bottles. This felt a little intrusive, but if it would help make Courtney's job easier, it was worth it. She seemed like a nice girl stuck in a really thankless situation.

After shutting the fridge, he made a beeline for the exit. He'd wiled away a good part of the day already, and his crew would be wondering what had happened to him.

Just as he reached for the door, it swung open and in walked Miss Bijou herself in an old-fashioned dress, her auburn hair pinned up fancy and her makeup overdone in an actressy sort of way.

"Oh." Her wide eyes gleamed as they raked him from head to toe and back again.

Adam tried not to interpret her expression. "Pardon me, ma'am." He removed his hat and gestured with it toward the kitchen. "I was just—"

"Are you the masseur I asked for?" She tilted him a long look as she swung out one hip.

His stomach bucked. "No, ma'am. I'm here to help Courtney."

"Oh." She straightened. "I didn't realize they'd given her an assistant."

"No, ma'am, not an assistant." He edged past her, keeping as much distance as he could. "Just doing her a favor."

"I see." Sidling into his path, she extended a dainty hand. "I'm Angela Bijou."

"I know." He fingered his hat, then gracelessly reached out to shake. "I'm Adam Greene, ma'am."

"Adam." She squeezed his hand and seemed to roll his name around in her mouth. "Courtney will have to get you a crew pass so security will know to let you on set whenever you like."

"Yes, ma'am." He reclaimed his hand from her grasp and reached for the doorknob. Feeling like Joseph fleeing from Potiphar's wife, he made his escape, taking the two steps in one bound. A few yards from his truck, he ran into Courtney on her way to the trailer.

Her eyes brimmed with concern when she saw him. "Is everything okay?"

"Fine." He looked up to see Angela Bijou leaning against the doorway of the trailer, sizing him up as if he were a prize bull. "I just met your boss."

"Oh." Following his line of sight, Courtney's words quivered with quiet alarm. "I'm so *sorry*."

A shiver surged up Courtney's spine as Angela ogled Adam from the doorway of her trailer. Her expression read like an open book, one with Fabio splayed across the cover.

Next to Courtney, Adam fidgeted uncomfortably. Somehow, he didn't strike her as the kind of guy who would enjoy being the blue-plate special at Café Man-eater.

She encouraged him toward his truck. "Thanks again for your help."

He nodded, taking the final few steps to the driver's side door. "Anytime."

His gaze lingered on Courtney just long enough to make her want to demand his definition of "anytime." Was that just a show of courtesy, or a subtle hint that he hoped to see her again? And why did Angela have to stand there looking as if she'd made her main course selection and he was it?

As the old green pickup bumped and rumbled from the lot, Courtney reluctantly turned to follow her boss into the trailer.

Angela stood at the mirror primping her wig. "So, tell me about the cowboy."

Heat scored Courtney's face. "Adam? Well, he—"

"He's adorable." Angela yanked out a tendril and forced it into a curl. "He'd make a nice diversion."

A constriction squeezed Courtney's chest. "A *diversion?*"

"You know—something to take my mind off the pressures of work. Besides, this is my first Western. A cowboy could help me get a feel for this character. What do you think?"

Courtney bristled, certain that the real answer to that would clinch her place in the unemployment line in no time. She needed to be tactful. "Um…great. But what about Mr. Caulfield?"

Angela rolled her eyes. "*Jeffrey?* He could stand to know he's not the only cowboy on the range, if you know what I mean."

The little hairs on the back of Courtney's neck stood on end. Could anybody really be that self-absorbed?

"Besides—" Angela took a large makeup brush and added some rouge to her already-too-made-up-for-the-1800s cheeks "—being seen with someone from the working class could be good for my reputation on this movie. Even though my character is from money, she's a simple country girl at heart. Yes, I think having my own cowboy would do me good." She put down the brush and looked directly at Courtney. "I need you to arrange a date with him."

Courtney's courage dropped into her sneakers. How could she possibly play matchmaker for the cowboy and the diva? Adam would never go for it, and Courtney would suffer the consequences.

She fumbled for a deflection. "Your water should be chilled."

"Fabulous." Delight lifted Angela's countenance. "Grab a bottle for me, would you? We need to make our plan for the cowboy. What's his name…Alan?"

"Adam." Courtney's throat tightened around the word.

"Right." Angela breezed out the door, a satisfied smile on her Barbie-doll-perfect face.

Courtney groaned. Adam was too down to earth to be toyed with…wasn't he? She had to think. He was so nice—maybe he'd play along just enough for Courtney to receive kudos for a job well done.

She grabbed a slightly chilled bottle from the fridge and moved toward the door. At least now she had a reason to talk to Adam again. She half smiled. And he *would* be a whole lot easier to locate than French mineral water.

Chapter 6

As Courtney's gaze swept across the front of the Victorian-style ranch house, she half expected J. R. Ewing to stride out the front door.

The sprawling structure looked even prettier than she'd imagined when she read the script—think Southfork Ranch overlaid with *Music Man*. Its wooden siding gleamed a luminous white, while interesting turrets, ornamental gingerbread trim and a vivid red, slanted roof gave it the authentic 1880s character the location scouts had needed. A porch swing shifted from the movement of the crew working on the wide wraparound porch, enticing Courtney to abandon the skimpy camp stool on which she now perched and stretch out in comfort.

A movement from a small second-story balcony over the front porch caught her attention. Lacy curtains fluttered behind a windowed door, then stilled. Courtney narrowed her eyes, but saw no more signs of life. Her imagination raced. She'd overheard that the house had been built in the 1800s and the original family had passed the ranch down through the generations. Apparently, the current matriarch lived here with her kids. What kind of people would live in an impressive house like this?

She scrutinized the area and took in a lungful of hay-infused air. Since Angela was inside the house waiting for the crew to finish prepping for her entrance, Courtney had nothing to do.

A whinny drew her attention to a gorgeous but weather-worn red barn that stood some distance from the house. In a large fenced-in area just in front of the barn, a beautiful black horse reared up, shaking its head at a cowboy wearing dusty blue jeans and a tan work shirt. Intrigued, Courtney stood and moved slowly toward the corral. As she grew closer, her heart rate quickened. *Adam.*

His back was to her, and she allowed her gaze to wander from his broad shoulders down to his narrow hips and long legs. He stood firm in brown cowboy boots even as the horse lifted her nose and let out another protestation.

"Whoa, Pepper. Easy, girl."

The soothing cadence of Adam's deep, husky voice brought a smile to Courtney's face and seemed to have a similar effect on the animal.

"Easy, Pepper." Adam held up a reassuring palm, reaching with the other hand for a rope, which hung from the horse's neck.

Much to Courtney's amusement, the animal took a step toward Adam, as if giving him permission to take hold of the rope. Inch by careful inch, Adam moved his palm toward her. Just as his fingers grazed the horse's forehead, he reached out with his other hand and grasped the rope.

Courtney's heart did a little pirouette. She glanced back at the crew guys, confirming that they were still busy setting up, and crossed to the outside of the corral.

Just as she opened her mouth to say something clever, her

foot sank into a soft spot in the ground and she felt herself falling. In a terrible instant, she knew exactly what was about to happen. As she landed with a *splat* in the mud, both hands sank nearly to the wrists. Adam whipped around, surprise coloring his stubble-shaded face. He hurdled over the fence and knelt behind her, hooking his hands under her arms, and raised her to her feet.

"You okay?" His voice sounded light, but concerned. Moving around to face her, he kept his hands on her elbows for just a few beats while she regained her footing.

"I...I think so." She looked down at herself, partly to conceal the fact that her cheeks were turning the same shade of red as the barn next to them. "I can't believe I did that. What a klutz."

"Hey, we've all done it." His hand still on her elbow, he guided her out of the muck. "It's pretty easy to fall out here if you're not wearing boots."

She simpered slightly. His laid-back manner helped to lessen her feelings of total humiliation. At least she wasn't trying to impress him, because she truly would have just blown it if that were the case. Feeling steadier, she faced him. Her pulse kicked it up another notch. "Thanks for the hand."

"No problem." He peered down at her mud-caked jeans. "Hey, I think we've got some clothes that will fit you out in the bunkhouse. It's guy stuff, but some of our hands are in high school. I'm pretty sure something would fit."

She glanced back at the set, where things still appeared to be a far cry from readiness. "That sounds good." Catching his eye, her stomach did a quiet somersault.

He started toward a small white structure that looked like the dollhouse version of the main house. Her nerves jumped. *This must be where he lives. Along with the other ranch hands.*

They stepped up onto the cute front porch and Adam pushed open the door. Moving aside, he gestured for her to enter the cozy living room. It was tidy and simply decorated in a Western motif.

Impressive. "This is what you call a 'bunkhouse'? I was expecting…you know…*bunks*."

He smiled that nice smile, the one with the dimple. "The bunks are actually through there." He aimed a thumb at a couple of doors that led off a hallway to the side of the living room. "Some of the guys live here year round, so it's great for it to feel like home."

She nodded and slipped off her mud-encrusted sneakers. She padded into the room as Adam disappeared through another door. Following, she admired not only the inviting feel of the kitchen, but the fact that a bunch of ranch hands managed to keep it so clean. She crossed to the double sink and washed the muck off her hands.

"This movie thing is crazy." Adam spoke from what appeared to be a mudroom. "Did you see what they did to the lawn? They *spray-painted* it. Like it wasn't green enough. And that's not the half of it. You should see what they've done on the inside of the house. The rooms they're using look like something out of *Lonesome Dove*."

Adam emerged, his arms full of clothing and a pair of cowboy boots. "You can change in the bathroom, just down the hall. If you bring out your muddy stuff, we can toss it in the washer."

Gingerly, she took the jeans and boots from him. She went into the bathroom and changed, pleased with what she saw in the mirror. She actually felt kind of stylish.

Gliding out into the living room, she did a little fashion-model twirl.

He whistled. "Hey, now. I have a better eye for size than I thought."

"Do I look like one of the guys?"

He ran a hand through his thick hair. "Believe me, the guys aren't nearly as cute."

Lucky for her, he headed for the kitchen and missed the blush that spread across her cheeks like a Malibu brush fire. *Cute?* A smile worked its way over her lips as she trailed after him.

Once they were in the enclosed back porch, he nodded toward a big work sink. "We can rinse your things off before we throw them in. I washed most of the mud off your shoes, but I assume they can go through the machine."

She dipped her chin, and followed his instructions. He cranked on the water and continued to scrub her shoes while she set to work on her jeans. A quiver danced up her spine as she noted that she was close enough to smell peppermint on his breath.

"So, you got your bottled water okay?"

She grinned, grateful for his easy conversation. "My *D'eau Douce* was here when I arrived this morning. Thank goodness." Her eyes rolled. "One of the teamsters trucked it in from the airport in Helena. The poor guy's been up since 4:00 a.m. just to make sure the star stays hydrated."

"You movie folks must be used to rising early. I noticed your crew here before dawn getting set up." He sprayed a brown spot on her shoe with something from a red bottle. "They start as early as we do."

She wrung out her jeans, then stepped around him to drop them into the machine. "I hope they're not interfering too much with your work."

"It's okay." He tossed the shoes on top of her jeans, then measured out some powdered detergent and sprinkled it on top. "I'm just hoping the novelty wears off for the guys pretty soon. Now that they've all gotten an eyeful of what a real movie star looks like, maybe they'll go back to focusing on their own work."

"I wouldn't bet on it. Angela Bijou has a way of drawing male attention to her wherever she goes."

He lowered the lid and turned some dials. "I guess that's what they call 'star power.'"

She nodded, uncomfortable at the reminder of her assignment. She might not get another opportunity to speak to Adam in private, and she was here to do a job, after all. Still, what a shame to ruin their nice conversation.

She swallowed hard and steadied her voice. "So, what do *you* think of Angela?"

He shrugged, leading her back to the kitchen. "She's good, I guess." He opened the really cool retro refrigerator. "Want a root beer?"

"Please." She calculated her words. "So, Monday is our day off."

"I know." He twisted the caps off a couple of brown bottles and handed her one. "I'm counting on it being nice and quiet around here."

"Right." She took a sip of the soda, a sickening feeling of guilt spoiling her enjoyment of its sweetness. "So, you're working then?"

"We pretty much work six days a week in the summer. Sunday's off, of course." He took a long swig from his bottle.

"Of course." She fumbled for the right words. Why couldn't she just be a professional and spit it out? "So, Ms. Bijou... Angela...won't be busy on Monday and I was wondering if you might have some free time...."

His eyes flashed from something that looked like fear to delight. Courtney's heart sank a little. Even though her job was at stake here, she had secretly hoped he'd laugh off the idea of spending time with Angela.

Instead, he seemed enthused. "Oh, well, that sounds real good. I mean, I could knock off a little early if the guys are productive."

"Great." Now all that remained was to sort out the details. "So...what do you do for fun around here?"

He thought for a moment. "How about horseback riding?"

"Horseback riding?" She almost laughed at the thought of Angela on a horse. She started to say "no," but she somehow blurted out, "Sounds perfect."

His eyes twinkled. "Maybe dinner after? Something casual?"

She bit her lip, feeling as if they should shake hands or something. Suddenly remembering herself, she checked her watch. "Oh, I really need to get back. They've probably started shooting by now and Ms. Bijou—"

"I need to get back, too." He leaned in. "Pepper is known to be a diva herself, to tell you the truth."

She smiled and stood. As they walked back toward the set, shame and sadness coiled together to form a knot in her throat. She felt terrible about her participation in this plan to lure Adam into Angela's web, but even worse that he didn't seem to mind.

A deep breath forced all emotion aside. She was just doing her job, after all. Besides, Angela would probably fire her anyway when she found out the planned activity for the cowboy rendezvous.

Adam's heart beat a little quicker than normal as he worked his way back to the big house. In spite of his trepidations about getting involved with Courtney, he liked that she was interested in spending time with him. Whatever her intentions, what was the worst that could happen? They'd have some fun, maybe strike up a friendship. They had a nice rapport together, and he should just enjoy that.

He walked into the kitchen and snickered. Janessa sat at the window peeking out between the curtains like a secret agent on a mission. He crept up behind her like he used to do when they were kids.

"Anything unusual going on out there?"

She jumped, putting her hand to her chest, then flashed

him a blistering glare. "You just about scared me out of my skin."

He laughed. Janessa had been the one who'd wanted this movie to shoot at the ranch and it was obvious she was more than a little starstruck.

"You'll never guess what happened." She spun full around in her chair, her dark ponytail snapping. "They had Angela Bijou make her entrance from our front door out onto the porch. She was waiting in our entry hall forever with hair and makeup folks and people with headsets. It was so awesome. Someone came in and asked me to get a glass of water for her and I did. I actually got to hand it to the person who handed it to her. Isn't that exciting?"

"Water in a glass?" He furrowed his brow. "And she *drank* it?"

Janessa frowned. "Of course she drank it. You're missing the point."

He chuckled. What a prima donna. That whole business about the bottled water had apparently been a big power play. Poor Courtney. It was just like when he had a wild filly to tame, except worse. At least his horses respected him.

Janessa went back to peering out the window. "Who was that girl I saw you talking to?"

He took a glass out of the cupboard and tried to sound casual. "Her name's Courtney. She's Miss Bijou's gal Friday."

She huffed. "Lucky gal."

"Yeah, *real* lucky." He filled his glass with water, then held a beat. "We're going horseback riding on Monday."

Her eyes lit up as she whipped around. "You have a *date?*"

He lifted a hand. "*Not* a date. Just horseback riding." Janessa and Mama were concerned that he didn't date more. Or at all, really. He didn't want to make this out to be more than it was.

Janessa leaned forward. "Who asked who?"

"What?"

"On the date. Did you ask her, or did she ask you?"

Uncomfortable with this line of questioning, he tried to downplay it. He and his sister were close, but he really didn't want to get into the complexity of his feelings. The last thing he wanted to do was admit that he might be getting in over his head. "She just mentioned that Monday is her day off, and the next thing I knew—"

"The conversation just naturally led to you asking her to go horseback riding."

He tried to clench back a grin. "Something sort of like that, yeah."

"Well I think it's great. It's about time my brother did something besides work and go to church."

He cast her a loving but playfully irritated glance. "I'm not sure it's that great. I mean, she's obviously not going to stick around here after the movie's done shooting. It doesn't make sense for me to start something that's got no future."

She folded her arms and gave him a long look. "Wow. You must really like her."

"I don't know—"

"You like her. If you didn't, you wouldn't be so worried."

He opened his mouth to argue, but no words came out. It was no use trying to fool Janessa. She knew him way too well.

Chapter 7

After parting ways with Adam, Courtney hurried around to the front of the house. Her heart quickened at the sight of Angela standing on the porch, engaged in a discussion with the director, Mr. Kingsley. Thinking quickly, Courtney darted over to her campstool and lifted an icy bottle of *D'eau Douce* from the cooler next to it. She stepped carefully to the edge of the set, making sure Angela could see her if she looked. With any luck, she'd assume Courtney had been there all along.

"I'm not getting Jessie's motivation here." Angela swung out a reedlike arm as her voice rose to an unnecessarily high volume. "She loves Cord, so why would she let him leave?"

Mr. Kingsley rubbed his chin and gave her a long blink. "It's spelled out in the dialogue, Angela—"

"Well, I'm not seeing it. We'll just have to change the dialogue." She wheeled around to charge down the porch steps, her clearly aggravated director in tow. "I don't care *what* century this is. I can't have her appearing to be so weak."

Courtney straightened as Angela neared. Following after her, Mr. Kingsley seemed to be practicing his yoga breathing.

"Fine," he said, exasperation barely concealed behind a smooth tone. "We'll take a short break while I convene with the writers."

"That would be lovely." Angela reached out as she approached Courtney and took the bottle from her hand. "I'll be in my trailer." She turned and patted Mr. Kingsley on his unshaven cheek. "Don't be too long."

As Mr. Kingsley veered off with a shake of his graying head, Angela took a swig of water and started toward her trailer. Courtney relished a long breath. It appeared that no one had noticed her absence while she was off talking to Adam, but she'd have to be careful not to get so sidetracked. Smiling to herself, she fell into step behind Angela.

"Court-*neeey.*"

Courtney stopped just short of slamming into Angela, who now stood there examining the bottle in her hand. "Yes, Ms. Bijou?"

"What is going on with my water?"

Oh, great. Had Angela figured out yesterday that something was wrong but was only now remembering to chew her out about it?

"I'm not sure I—"

"This bottle just doesn't taste as good as yesterday's. What's the deal?"

Courtney stared at the bottle Angela held up at face level. There was no way she could have accidentally given her one they'd filled at the well, because Angela had downed the last of those last night. The bottle she held in her hand was from the case that had been delivered that morning. *D'eau Douce*—the real thing.

It slowly dawned on Courtney that Angela's complaint wasn't with the makeshift well water, but with the stuff that had been jetted in straight from France, via the Von's in L.A.

She pulled in a relieved breath, even though she still brooked Angela's angry demand for an explanation. "It tasted better yesterday?"

Angela held the bottle out in front of her as if it repulsed her. "You'd better explain this to me."

Courtney thought fast. "There have been studies of spring water that say the taste is affected by the mineral content, which can change daily. Most people don't have discerning enough palates to detect the subtle difference."

"Oh." Angela's heated expression dropped, and she took a delicate sip from her bottle. "Well, I *am* very discriminating."

Courtney gave her a reassuring smile, making a mental note—when in doubt, stroke the diva's ego.

As Angela recommenced walking, Courtney fell into a confident half step back. "So, I have news about Adam."

"Oh?" Angela's carefully shaped eyebrows arched. "Do tell."

"You have a date with him on Monday."

"Wonderful." Her sultry visage faded to uncertainty. "What will I wear?" She pointed the bottle at Courtney. "Go online and find me the perfect outfit in a size zero. Prada or Armani, you choose."

Courtney braced herself. "How about Straus?"

"Straus?"

"As in 'Levi.'"

"What?"

"See…" Courtney gave her words careful consideration. "Adam is a *cowboy* and he wants to take you horseback rid-ing."

Angela's eyes widened with horror as she stopped short and stared at Courtney. "*Horse*back riding? But wouldn't that involve *touching* one of those filthy creatures?"

Courtney shrugged. "Unless someone's figured out a dif-ferent way to do it."

"Impossible." She reached for the door of her trailer. "I've never ridden a horse before. I might break a bone…or a nail. I might…" Her eyes lit up. "Whose idea was this?"

"Well, Adam said that—"

"And you agreed, right?"

"Uh…yes, but—"

"Courtney, you're brilliant. Remind me to give you one of those things people give for good service."

"A tip?"

"Yes, one of those." Angela stepped into the trailer. "You might not believe this, but I've never actually been on a horse before."

Courtney followed her inside. "No?"

"No." Crossing straight to the makeup table, Angela sat down and started to primp. "*N2M* is my first Western, and my character, Jessie, doesn't have any riding scenes."

Courtney nodded, as if this was news to her.

"Of course, *Jeffrey* has several, and he can't even get on the thing. Do you know why?"

Edging closer to her boss, Courtney laced her fingers together.

Angela lowered her voice conspiratorially. "He's afraid of animals. All kinds."

"Oh." Wincing, Courtney recalled the scene in *The Pharaoh's Tomb* where he had shared a canteen with a camel. "That must be…inconvenient."

"Who cares?" Angela's bowlike mouth twisted. "Anyway, you'll go with me in case I have any trouble."

Anxiety wedged in Courtney's throat. "You want me to go *with* you?"

Angela waved a hand. "I know Monday is your day off, but what else is there to do in this town?"

I don't know. Courtney wanted to cry. *Laundry. Sleep.* "What do you need me to *do?*"

"Well, since I've never ridden before, I might need you to

help. When I'm ready to be alone with the cowboy, I'll dismiss you. Got it?"

She nodded, her smile weak. She wasn't sure which she dreaded more—going on the date with Angela and Adam, or leaving them alone together. The thought of both made her stomach hurt.

Seated next to Angela in the back of the Lincoln Town Car, Courtney stared out at the blur of trees and pondered a means of escape that wouldn't involve severe bodily harm. What was she doing here? Angela had probably been on enough dates in her life to impress even Mr. Guinness. Why did she need Courtney along? Besides, the closer they got to the ranch, the more embarrassed Courtney became. This setup just felt so awkward.

It didn't help that Angela looked like a million bucks in the perfect outfit Courtney had internet-shopped for her. Although the off-the-shoulder, fuchsia Marrika Nakk stretch-velvet top wouldn't have been Courtney's first choice, it did accentuate both Angela's Barbie-doll shape and her movie-star status.

As Angela stretched out her mile-long legs in her vintage Levi's, a pang of regret jabbed Courtney in the ribs. Why had she talked Angela out of the less form-hugging tiered-chiffon skirt she had seen on a Western wear designer's website, just because it would be impractical for riding?

"But the model is on a horse," Angela had protested.

"The model is *lying* on a horse," Courtney had responded. "And that was most likely Photoshopped."

Now, Courtney glanced down at her own scrawny figure in the same borrowed jeans and boots from the other day, which she'd paired with a pink T-shirt she'd owned since college. Adam *had* called her "cute" but she was definitely Mary Ann to Angela's Ginger. The only upside to Angela's alluring outfit was that Adam most likely wouldn't even notice Courtney was there.

"Remember—" Angela took out a compact and checked her lipstick "—I need you to help keep the horse under control."

"Okay...." *Keep the horse under control? Who does she think she's talking to, Annie Oakley?* "But I've never ridden before, either—"

"Tell me..." Ignoring Courtney's protestation, Angela pivoted slightly in her seat, holding her arms out mannequin style. "How do I look?"

"F-fine." Courtney rolled in her lips. No wonder Angela commanded somewhere in the neighborhood of $10 million a movie—she was stunning. Flawless skin, perfect white teeth, eyes the color of emeralds. Her platinum hair fell in soft curls from under the black rhinestone-studded cowgirl hat that had been overnighted from Texas for an astronomical price and was a perfect match with the Austrian crystal-drenched belt with the rhinestone buckle.

Poor Adam didn't stand a chance. Courtney blinked back a surge of emotion she felt reluctant to admit to.

As the car rolled down the long drive past the ranch house, Courtney glanced up. Adam led two beautiful brown horses out of the barn and lifted his chin toward the car in greeting.

The driver eased into the area next to the corral, then got out to open the door for Angela. Languidly, she swung one black hand-tooled-leather-booted foot out of the car, then the other. The rest of her body followed, as though she were stepping onto a red carpet instead of a gravel driveway.

"Hello, handsome." She jutted out a hip as Adam approached the car.

Courtney unobtrusively slipped out the other side. Adam's eyes met hers, confusion flitting across his face. No doubt he was thinking three's a crowd and wondering what she was doing on his date with the rodeo princess. If only she could explain that she'd disappear later, allowing the privacy he'd no doubt been counting on.

"I hope you have a horse for each of us." Angela looked coyly at the animals in the yard next to them.

"Oh, so you're *both* riding then?" His tone was hard to read—puzzled, but maybe a little amused.

Courtney chimed in as she made her way around the car. "It's just that Angela's never ridden before"

"*N2M* is my first Western." Angela tossed her hair over her shoulder in a well-rehearsed move that had probably clinched the deal in more than one audition.

The corners of Adam's eyes crinkled as he looked from Angela to Courtney. "I don't mind giving lessons." Looking again at Angela, he gestured toward one of the horses behind them. "We'll put you on Miss Molly. She's gentle as a lamb."

"Oh, I just love lamb." Angela guardedly glided toward the fence and held out her hand in the direction of the horses.

Clasping her elbows, Courtney inched closer to Adam and leaned in. "Sorry about this, I—"

"No worries." He held up a hand. "I totally get your situation."

She forced a little smile. He *got* it? She didn't even completely get it herself.

"She likes you," he called over to Angela, as she tentatively allowed Miss Molly to nuzzle her hand.

Angela looked unsure.

Adam bent down and grabbed a hunk of long grass, then crossed to Angela. "Try feeding her this. She loves it."

Eying the grass as if it might bite her, Angela took it. She held it up to Miss Molly, who enthusiastically gripped it in her teeth. Angela looked startled, then eased into an uncertain smile.

Though he still addressed Angela, Adam gave Courtney a wink. "You two just keep getting acquainted while I get another horse ready." A grin crooked one side of his mouth as he glanced at Courtney and tipped his head toward the barn.

Courtney double-checked that Angela was occupied with the horse, then followed Adam. Inside, he went straight to a wall filled with horse paraphernalia and grabbed a big brush.

Her gut knotted. She'd better take advantage of her minute alone with him to explain the situation. "Ms. Bijou is used to having me with her—"

"Don't even worry about it." He nodded toward one of the stalls. "I'll have you ride Pepper. All the other horses are out with my hands rounding up the cattle."

"Pepper?" She looked at the gorgeous black animal. "Isn't she the one I saw you with the other day? The one with the attitude?"

"She's a bit of a handful." He winked as he opened the gate to the stall. "But, hey, if anyone knows how to deal with a prima donna, it's you."

A smile crept across her face as she watched him brush and saddle up the horse, her self-consciousness about being there slowly melting away.

Chapter 8

An hour or so later, Courtney felt totally at ease with Pepper. Adam had given her a few pointers and left her to ride around the corral while he worked with Angela, who wasn't faring quite so well.

"Are you sure I'm not going to fall off?" It was hard to tell if the tremble in her voice resulted from fear or Miss Molly's lively gait.

"You won't fall." Adam's strong voice reassured her.

As if on cue, Miss Molly stopped abruptly, sending Angela lurching forward. She made an *ooooph* sound as her eyes bugged to twice their normal size.

Adam's face creased with restrained mirth. "You okay?" As he glanced Courtney's way, she couldn't help sending him a sly smirk.

"I'm fine." Angela raised her torso and blew a wayward strand of hair off her forehead. "I'm just not used to doing my own driving."

Courtney giggled to herself as poor Angela struggled. Her

hands clenched the reins so tightly, she looked like she might cut off her own circulation.

"Just pretend you're riding a bicycle." Adam tossed Courtney a wink.

Angela huffed. "Do I look like a woman who would ride a *bicycle?*"

Miss Molly rolled her head, as if to express her own amusement. Angela shot the horse a look that implied she wasn't pleased at having to deal with a creature so ill-equipped to obey her every whim without question.

The sound of crackling gravel caught Courtney's attention, and she turned to see a large and impressive bronze-colored pickup truck kicking up dust on its way down the driveway.

Adam turned serious. "'Scuse me a minute, ladies." He left the corral, meeting the truck as it pulled up next to the house.

Courtney was vaguely aware of Angela battling to get Miss Molly to move as a man got out of the truck and shook Adam's hand. Courtney's pulse instantly accelerated. She couldn't believe it.

Ever since high school, she'd dreamed of working with Travis Bloom. He was one of the world's most important directors, as big as Spielberg. She'd plotted a hundred different ways she could "happen" to meet him, and here he was, not fifty feet away. What in the world was he doing here?

"How do I get off this thing?"

Courtney glanced at Angela, then encouraged Pepper to close the gap between them. "Well, I—"

"Do you know who that is?" Angela spoke in an urgent, hushed tone. "That's Travis Bloom. *The* Travis Bloom."

"I know. Do you have any idea why he—"

"All he had to do was have his people call my agent and set up lunch at the Ivy. He didn't have to come all the way out here to the edge of the middle of nowhere."

Courtney quirked a brow. Judging from the intense conversation Mr. Bloom was having with Adam, she doubted he had come here just to meet Angela.

Clicking her tongue, Courtney prodded Pepper to move to the fence. To her amazement, Miss Molly followed.

Adam looked up as they drew closer, the somber expression on his face taking Courtney by surprise. He said something to Mr. Bloom and the two of them approached the fence.

Dressed in tan khakis and a periwinkle polo shirt, Mr. Bloom looked even more distinguished in person than in print. He wore his salt-and-pepper hair cropped short, and his beard neatly trimmed. He looked good for a guy who'd suffered the stress and strain of putting together more than twenty-five blockbusters in as many years.

"Ladies—" Adam's voice was more subdued than it had been earlier "—this is Travis Bloom. Mr. Bloom, I'd like you to meet Courtney—"

"—Jacobs, sir. Courtney Jacobs." Her heart pounded so hard, it felt as if a marimba band had invaded her chest. She started to stick out her hand, then realized she was too far away to expect him to shake it, and jerked it back.

Mr. Bloom smiled cordially. "Ms. Jacobs."

Adam gestured toward Angela. "And this is Angela—"

"Help me down, Adam." Angela's impatience showed through the patina of her well-practiced smile.

Adam went through the gate, then reached out a hand to help her.

She took a moment to get her footing on the soft ground, then sauntered out of the corral, her hand outstretched. "Travis. I'm so pleased to finally meet you. Your work is genius. Simply genius."

He looked surprisingly humble. "And I've long been an admirer of yours as well, Ms. Bijou. It's a pleasure to cross paths."

Her eyes dropped to the muck under their feet. "Perhaps

we should go over there, where our paths aren't quite so... *fragrant*."

Mr. Bloom looked to Adam, who nodded as if to signify their conversation was complete. Angela took the older man by the arm and walked with him toward his truck.

Courtney bit her lip. No wonder Angela had gotten so far in this business, with moxie like that. Courtney was way too self-conscious to attempt that kind of schmoozing.

She looked down at Adam whose mind seemed to be elsewhere.

"Umm...I think I'm going to need your help, too."

His gaze slid slowly upward. "Oh. Right. Sorry."

As he held out both hands, she grabbed hold of the saddle horn and swung her leg to the ground. Once both feet were secure, she turned to face him. "That was fun."

He smiled, though his jaw still seemed a little tight. "You're a natural." He looked over at Mr. Bloom's truck, where Angela was speaking to him animatedly. "It looks like the riding lesson is over."

"She's pretty excited to meet him. I guess she just got distracted."

"Seems like it." He paused. "So, do you think she'll want to hang out, or—"

"Oh, I'm sure of it." This was awkward. "Hang out. Or something."

He gave a slow nod. His face had softened, but was still hard to read.

Courtney shifted uncomfortably. Of course he wanted her to get lost, but she couldn't leave without Angela's permission. Since she didn't dare interrupt her boss's conversation with one of the most important men in show business, there she was—sandwiched between a rock and a hard place.

"So—" the lightheartedness tried to return to his tone "—it looks like maybe this would be a good time for you and me to—"

"Excuse the interruption." Mr. Bloom walked toward them like a man who had important things to do. He offered his hand to Adam. "Thank you for the information, son. I'll have my lawyer get back to you in a day or two."

His lawyer? Courtney sent Adam a glance, but sensed she'd be out of place in asking.

"Ms. Jacobs."

Eyes widening, she stared at the hand Mr. Bloom now extended to her. Jolting to her senses, she grabbed it a little too exuberantly. "It was a pleasure, sir." Why had she just called him "sir"? It wasn't as if he were *that* old. Had she just insulted him?

After Mr. Bloom headed for his truck, Courtney noticed the driver opening the door to the backseat of the Town Car for Angela. What was going on?

Courtney spoke to Adam over her shoulder as she started toward the car. "Excuse me a sec."

She arrived just after Angela had gotten in and rolled down the window.

Angela's eyes sparkled with excitement. "He has a script he wants to discuss. I'm meeting him for dinner."

"Oh." Courtney's stomach pinged. "But, you were supposed to have dinner with Adam."

Angela raised her thin, blond brows. "Courtney, this is *Travis Bloom.* Just tell Mr. Gorgeous I'll have to give him a rain check on dinner. He'll understand, I'm sure."

Courtney suppressed a smile. She only hoped that Adam wouldn't be too disappointed.

"Hurry up and tell him." Angela waved her toward Adam. "I need to shower and change before dinner."

"Right." Courtney fairly skipped back to where Adam tended to the horses.

He looked up. "She decided not to stick around?"

"I guess Mr. Bloom wants to talk to her about a script. She doesn't want to miss the opportunity, so…"

"I see." He nodded. "She's pretty career driven."

"That's what got her where she is." She glanced toward the car. "Look, I'm really sorry about dinner."

His brow furrowed. "Don't tell me she expects you to leave, too?"

"*Oh.* Well…"

"It *is* your day off, right?"

She looked again at the car. "I suppose so."

"So, unless you have to leave for some other reason, let's go for the trail ride I planned."

Courtney's mouth froze around her compulsory refusal, leaving her lost in those dazzling brown eyes. It *was* her day off, and she was having fun. What would be the harm in soaking up some local color? Especially when the local in question was so charming and appealing.

She gave up a restrained smile. "I'll just let Ms. Bijou know."

As Adam led the way up the trail on Rocky, he glanced back at Courtney, who seemed to be handling Pepper like a pro. He chuckled to himself. Movie people were a different breed, that was for sure, but Courtney seemed normal. Almost as if she belonged here.

They shared a comfortable silence as they rode. He still didn't quite get why Angela had come with her on their date, but it didn't matter now. He might as well add "distracting Angela from playing chaperone" to the growing list of things for which he was grateful to Travis Bloom.

He angled his head slightly so Courtney could hear him. "We're just about there."

"Where's 'there'?" Her manner sounded carefree.

He lobbed a grin over his shoulder. "You'll see."

As the horses clopped up the trail, the distant sound of birds calling to each other echoed through the woods covering the mountainside above and below. Evening sun flickered between limbs of ancient pines, the scent of which hung in the air.

They rounded the final bend and the expanse of the valley opened up before them. The mountains rolled from green to a distant faded blue, where they met the softening pink of the horizon. A smile tugged at the corner of his mouth. This was a view he would never get tired of.

Courtney gasped. "Oh…it's so beautiful." She stopped her horse beside his. "I've never seen so much *nature*."

He laughed. "You don't have nature where you live?"

"Some, but it's mostly covered in golf courses and housing developments." She tipped him a glance. "Why hasn't that happened here?"

He swung off his horse. "Well, for one thing, the Bar-G covers a good six thousand acres. Beyond that, you're seeing some other ranches and private property. That mountain range is protected by the federal land act, so no one's going to build on it except birds and tree squirrels." He tied both horses' reins to a fallen tree and stepped over to help Courtney dismount.

Her feet on the ground, she gave a long stretch and rubbed her back.

Keeping an eye on her, he crossed to Rocky. "You doing okay?"

"Oh, great." She sent him an unhurried smile. "I'm more relaxed than I've felt in days. It's been a rough week."

Adam reached for his saddlebag, pulled out a blanket and spread it on a level patch of ground. "You enjoy working for such an unpredictable boss?"

"I enjoy what I do." She paused, as if choosing her words with care. "Angela's a challenge."

He clucked at the obvious understatement. Placing the saddlebag down on the blanket, he gestured for her to sit.

She obliged. "What's this?"

He sat next to her. "Dinner."

She watched as he removed a few plastic containers and set them on the blanket in front of them. "Wow. Don't tell me you know how to cook?"

"Hey, we work up an appetite out on the range. It can't hurt to know a few basics."

Lifting a corner of one of the lids, she peeked in. "So, corn bread, and…" Picking up another container, she eyed it warily. "What's this?"

"A local delicacy." He grinned. "Ever had fried rattle-snake?"

She dropped the container and held her hands up in surrender.

He chuckled. "I'm kidding. It's fried chicken."

Relief washed over her pretty face. "Well, I have to say I'm very impressed. You really went all out here." Her nose scrunched. "Sorry the date didn't go as expected."

He smiled, pleased that she had thought of it as a date, but treading lightly. "Hey, all that matters now is that you're getting away from the stress of your job."

Her glance shifted sideways. "I hope you didn't mind giving us a lesson."

"Naw. It's been a while since I taught anyone to ride."

"From what I can tell, you're a natural teacher."

"Thanks. I'd do it more if I had time. The ranch keeps me so busy I'm scrambling to get all my work done as it is." He stopped himself, not wanting to complain. His gaze traveled across the valley. "I can't imagine a more relaxing place in this whole world."

Leaning back, she grabbed hold of her knees. The little lines that had creased her forehead earlier in the day had smoothed. He smiled to himself.

"Oh, I almost forgot." Reaching out, he took a thermos from the saddlebag, then unscrewed the cup and handed it to her. "May I pour?"

Curiosity crossed her face. "What is it?"

"Specialty of the house." He filled her cup full of clear liquid. "I call it 'Faux *Douce*.' I'm considering bottling it and selling it to people in foreign countries. They'll think it's exotic."

She giggled and took a sip. Her expression shifted. "Oooo, that really *is* good. No wonder Angela liked this better."

"I could have told you. No point in spending all that money. God has provided the sweetest water on earth for us right here."

She seemed to consider his words and took another drink.

Adam opened the rest of the containers. "Dig in. It's nothing fancy."

Picking up a piece of chicken, she contemplated the view. "It's perfect." She met and held his gaze. "All of it."

Uneasiness prickled his skin. It did seem just perfect.

Eager for a distraction, he swept his attention across the valley. "See that place up there—where the side of the mountain levels out?" He pointed to a nearby rim.

"You mean where it looks like a shelf?"

"Yeah. It's called Eternity Ridge. That's probably my favorite place in this whole world."

"Oh, really?" Grabbing a piece of corn bread, her eyes seemed to sparkle. "Why's that?"

"You can see across four counties from there." He hesitated. Why was he telling her this? "It's where my mama and dad had their wedding."

"No kidding?" She pointed. "Way up there?"

"Uh-huh. I don't go there much. It's kinda...special." He considered. "I'll take you up there sometime, if you'd like." Had he really said that? He'd never suggested that to anybody before. What was it about this girl?

Serenity tinted her pretty eyes. "I'd like that a lot. If you think I'm up to the ride."

"An old hand like you?" He elbowed her arm.

She teasingly bumped him with her knee, sending warmth

through him like he'd never experienced before. He mentally pinched himself. Not only did this girl not live in Thornton Springs, but he didn't even know if she was a Christian. It was totally irresponsible of him just being here with her.

That thought drifted off and an odd contentment settled in its place. He smiled and picked up a drumstick. Who but the good Lord Himself knew what He had in store?

Chapter 9

"Where's my breath spray?" Angela stood next to Jeffrey on the front porch of the ranch house, face tilted toward a makeup lady and hand outstretched.

Rising a little too quickly, Courtney grimaced. A surge of pain careened through every overexerted muscle in her body. She grabbed the spray from Angela's bag and tried to force herself to move normally. Every action felt like torture. Who knew that horseback riding could provide such a full-body workout?

At the bottom step, she took in a deep breath. This was not going to be fun. As she hoisted up her foot, a movement hooked the corner of her eye. Adam, carrying a couple of wood planks from the barn, grinned and shook his head at her. She shot him a playful glare and hoisted herself up another step. Of course *he* wasn't sore this morning.

"Courtney! My spray." Angela waved her hand, still unable to turn away from the powder puff in her face.

Forcing a fortitude she did not feel, Courtney bolted up the steps, handed the bottle to Angela and fired a so-there look at Adam. He responded with an even bigger grin.

"Clear the set. Places, everyone!" The assistant director's warning initiated a scurry of activity from the porch.

As the makeup artist hurried away, Courtney retrieved the bottle from Angela, who prevented her leaving with a grab of her wrist. *Youch.* Even that part of her hurt.

Angela tossed a half look in Jeffrey's direction. "Was Adam terribly disappointed yesterday?"

Jeffrey tilted his head as he adjusted his cuff button.

"A little." Courtney kept her voice low. "But he understood, just like you said."

"Good." Angela clearly intended to be heard. "Tell him I'll more than make it up to him soon."

Courtney forced a stiff nod. Angela dropped Courtney's wrist so abruptly that the spray bottle popped from her grasp, rolled and came to a stop next to Jeffrey's steel-toed boot.

"What's going on up there? Clear the set!" Although Keith Kingsley bellowed loud enough to be heard in the next county, he somehow felt the need to use the megaphone, anyway.

Suddenly paralyzed by a potent tonic of pain and humiliation, Courtney looked from the silent crew gaping up at her to the wayward bottle at Jeffrey Mark Caulfield's feet. The very thought of taking those few steps and bending down made her want to consider a career change. Mr. Kingsley raised a threatening eyebrow and an image of herself on the next plane home flashed through Courtney's mind.

Just as she was about to power through the painful movement, Jeffrey bent to pick up the bottle, then handed it to her.

Gratitude surged through her aching form. "Thank you."

"Don't mention it," he said with a wink of one of his famous silvery-blue eyes.

Angela tsked. "You're keeping her from doing her job, Jeffrey." She whirled toward Courtney. "Keith said to clear the set."

Biting her lip in lieu of a bullet, Courtney scurried down the steps and eased herself onto her campstool.

"Roll film...action!"

Angela gazed up into Jeffrey's eyes. If the Academy of Motion Picture Arts and Sciences could have witnessed her instant transformation from ticked-off leading lady to adoring heroine, she would win an Oscar for sure.

With one eyebrow raised á la Clark Gable, Jeffrey spoke his first line. "Jessie, I'll come back for you. I promise."

"I know you will, Cord." She twisted her hands in front of her and batted her long lashes. "You always keep your promises."

Taking her by the shoulders, he gave her a long, lingering kiss.

Courtney watched in fascination. Nobody had ever kissed *her* like that. How could actors make it seem so realistic?

"And cut!" Mr. Kingsley shouted into the megaphone.

Angela pushed away from Jeffrey. "Ugh. What part of 'don't grab me so hard' do you need defined?"

"I'm barely touching you." Jeffrey rolled his eyes and turned as the makeup lady charged toward him with a cotton ball aimed at his mouth. "As it is, I have to overcompensate for the passion of the moment with my reading of the line."

"Passion?" Angela spoke with stilled lips as another makeup artist dabbed at her with a brush. "You wouldn't know passion if it bit you on the face."

"Hrmph." His mouth apparently free of any trace of Angela's lipstick, Jeffrey took a water bottle from his assistant. "It's called 'acting,' darling. Something you might like to try sometime."

Courtney could have sworn she saw smoke come out of Angela's ears. They were both acting, all right. Acting like a couple of kids.

Twelve takes later, Courtney had been up and down the steps so many times her legs felt numb, but it was probably better than sitting still. They had finally made it to the end of the scene, where Jeffrey's character, Cord, rides off on his trusty horse after kissing Jessie.

"…and…action!"

Releasing Angela from the kiss, Jeffrey trudged boldly from the porch toward the waiting horse, which the wrangler held just out of the shot. Looking extremely ill at ease, Jeffrey grabbed the saddle horn and started to lift his foot to the stirrup.

"And cut!" Mr. Kingsley's voice was no less grating even when he appeared pleased. "Perfect, kids. Let's move on. Where's my riding double?"

A man dressed identically to Jeffrey sprang to his feet and switched places with him. Mr. Kingsley bellowed "Action!" and Jeffrey's twin mounted the horse and rode away.

From the corner of her eye, Courtney watched Jeffrey plunk down in his canvas chair and take a swig of water. She felt a little sorry for him, being unable to do his own riding. He had, after all, jumped from a burning building in *The Dark Bandit,* and scaled a sheer rock wall in *Final Vengeance.* It wasn't like he was a wimp or anything.

Angela leaned against the porch railing, watching the stunt double ride out of the shot. As soon as the director yelled "Cut!" she pushed herself upright and stormed down the steps.

"This is embarrassing. Why does Jeffrey get to look all macho and heroic when he can't even get on the horse?"

Sighing audibly, Mr. Kingsley stood and met her at the base of the stairs. "What can we do to make you happy here, Angela?"

Reluctantly, Courtney joined the throng of technicians who swarmed around the star like bees.

"I want a riding scene."

"A what?"

"A scene where I ride a horse. I think Jessie needs to show that she's tough and capable. After all, she's fighting to save her ranch, isn't she? She has to show that she's a match for the men. Jeffrey's character rides a horse. Why shouldn't mine?"

Jeffrey, who had been sitting with his hat in his lap and his feet elevated, leaped up and charged toward them. "Don't fall for it, Keith. She's only trying to make me look bad."

"Oh, like you need my help with that." Angela folded her arms and shot him a scalding glare.

A tiny bead of sweat trickled down Mr. Kingsley's forehead as he looked from Angela to Jeffrey, seeming to weigh the consequences of favoring one star over the other. His eyes landed on Angela. "We'll write something in."

"Aw…." Jeffrey tossed back his head and stomped to his chair.

Mr. Kingsley continued. "Give us a day or two to sort out the specifics. In the meantime—"

"In the meantime, I can start taking lessons." A small smile played on Angela's lips.

"Lessons…right…." Mr. Kingsley rubbed his craggy brow and directed his words to the A.D.—crew speak for "assistant director." "Talk to the wrangler about teaching Angela to—"

"Not that *idiot.*" Angela drew a long lean arm in the direction of the corral where Adam was examining a broken rung on the fence. *"Him."*

"Him?" Mr. Kingsley's eyes grew large. "But, he doesn't even work for us. He's the—"

"I need someone I'm comfortable with. Otherwise, it will never work and we might as well forget the whole picture."

A bird cawed breaking the silence that otherwise settled over the yard. Courtney's heart raced and she fought the urge to blurt out that this was just a ploy to manipulate more time with Adam. If Mr. Kingsley said yes, it would encourage Angela to continue to make ridiculous demands, and put Adam on the spot. He didn't have time to teach lessons. He'd said so himself.

"Fine." Mr. Kingsley wiped his hand across his eyes. "I'll have my A.D. work out a schedule."

Courtney's chest squeezed. Why couldn't anybody say no around here?

"*She'll* arrange it." Angela waved a hand toward Courtney. "She knows the cowboy."

Mr. Kingsley regarded Courtney with a defeated air that communicated both approval and solidarity. "Fine. Just talk to the A.D. and make sure he gets a contract signed." He looked again at Angela. "Now, can we get back to today's shooting schedule?"

Angela gave a nonchalant shrug and sauntered to her chair.

As the crew disbanded to set up the next shot, Mr. Kingsley bent in close to Courtney. "Just tell the cowboy we'll pay him double the going rate for riding lessons. Anything for the movie."

Courtney looked at Adam, still inspecting his fence, and rehearsed how to talk him into this. *Anything for the movie.*

Adam rubbed his jaw as he surveyed the broken fence. It was just a couple of boards, but if he didn't fix it today, he might not get to it till next week. He'd fallen behind on his work as it was, thanks to the movie. With the guys out tending to their own chores all day and him not able to make any noise around the cameras, things could go downhill real fast. As if life around here wasn't tough enough.

He looked up as Courtney hobbled toward him, doing a poor job of concealing her sore riding muscles. His mood shifted. At least one thing in his life right now felt uplifting.

"Hey." Stopping on the outside of the fence, she offered him about the prettiest smile he'd ever seen.

"Hey, yourself." Not very original, but at least he hadn't made a dumb joke.

She studied the boards propped against the fence. "We're

between shots now if you need to, you know, *hammer* anything."

He smiled lightly, appreciating the acknowledgment of his plight. "No, I think I'll wait. I'm a little afraid of that guy yelling at me through his bullhorn again."

She nodded, clearly remembering the other day when filming had stopped because he had misjudged his timing in bringing Pepper out to graze. It had been humiliating having the entire cast and crew staring at him.

Draping her arms over the top rung of the fence, she watched him measure one of the boards.

He flicked her a quick look, sensing that this was more than just a casual visit.

"So, I was wondering…" She wavered, as if her thought hadn't yet fully formed.

A grin found his lips. "Yes?"

"Remember when we were out riding, and you said that you—"

"Hey, Adam!"

Both their heads snapped in the direction of the trail from the backcountry. One of his lead hands galloped toward them with an urgency that made Adam jerk to attention.

"Yeah, Leonard?" he called out as the man neared.

"We got us a drainage problem out in the north pasture. I thought you'd want to get on it as soon as possible."

Adam heaved out a breath. *What next?* "Thanks for telling me."

Leonard tipped his hat toward Courtney—at least his guys knew to acknowledge the presence of a lady—and turned his horse around, heading back from where he'd come.

Lifting his eyebrows, Adam gave Courtney a resigned look. "So much for the fence." He tucked his tape measure into his toolbox and flipped the lid shut.

"Oh." Something sounding like disappointment tinged her voice. "Will you be gone all day?"

"Could be. Depends on how bad the problem is." He stood and faced her. If he could have his way, he'd stay and wile away the afternoon with her, but they both had work to do. "You were about to ask me a question?"

Her eyes opened a little wider, as if he'd reminded her of something she wasn't quite confident about putting voice to. "Oh…uh…it can wait."

That small hesitation made him all the more determined to drag it out of her. Eyes narrowing, he leaned on the fence across from her. "Now, after all the effort it took for you to limp over here, it would be ungentlemanly of me not to give you a chance to say your piece."

She jabbed her thumb in the direction of Leonard's exit. "But don't you have to go?"

He lifted a palm. "A minute more won't hurt. What did you want to ask me?"

"Would you mind…" Pausing, her gaze skimmed past his shoulder to where the horses grazed. "Is it all right if I give Pepper an apple from crafts service? I'm trying to win her over."

"An apple?" He snickered, wondering what she had *really* wanted to ask. "Sure. But don't worry about winning her over. I think she's already smitten." His mouth lifted as he bent to pick up the tool box.

Smitten. Yeah. He had to admit it. Pepper wasn't the only one.

Chapter 10

"How can I possibly choose? They're *both* so cute." Standing in the living room of her trailer, Angela jutted out a slender hip as she studied the two dresses Courtney held up on hangers.

Courtney gritted her teeth to keep from shouting, "Just decide!" It was only for the car ride back to the house where they were staying in town. Who cared if she wore Vera Wang or Nicole Miller?

Shifting her weight, Courtney tried to suppress her rumbling stomach. All she wanted was to grab a sandwich at the diner and attack her laundry. She hadn't been able to put on a clean pair of jeans in five days.

Just as Angela grabbed the Vera Wang, the doorbell pinged. "Tell them to go away!" she barked over her shoulder and retreated toward the bedroom.

"It's me, Ms. Bijou." The voice of the PR woman—Jody?—sounded through the closed front door. Courtney shot a contrite wince in the direction of Angela's departure and went to open it.

Jody, if that was her name, wore a look of apology that melted into bland irritation at the sight of Courtney. Balancing a stack of eight-by-ten photos of Angela in her arms, she called into the room. "I'm sorry to bother you, Ms. Bijou, but I have a favor to ask." She held a beat before adding. "For the movie."

Angela, now dressed, strutted from the bedroom to the makeup table. "Well?"

Jody stepped inside and plunked the pile of glamorous glossies onto the coffee table. "The Montana Children's Welfare League is hosting a fund-raiser showing of *Princess Pricilla* in Helena tomorrow morning. I just found out about it." She shifted nervously. "Kids love you in that movie."

Angela smoothed her hair and smiled at her image in the mirror. "Of course they do."

"The league would like you to make a personal appearance." Jody couldn't quite suppress the nervous quiver in her voice. "It would be great publicity for *N2M*."

"Tomorrow's Wednesday." Angela frowned. "Am I available?"

Jody wrung her hands, probably without realizing it. "Keith is willing to work around it."

"I don't know." Bending closer to the mirror, Angela stroked her impossibly thick eyelashes with her index finger. "Would I have to *do* anything?"

"No, not really." Jody sounded more confident than she appeared. "Just say hello to the kids from the stage before the movie. And—" a hint of the quiver returned "—they'd like to hand out an autographed photo to each child." Her eyes lowered to the stack of headshots. "They can be signed in advance, of course."

"Of course." Angela reached for her tube of cranberry-colored lip gloss. "No big deal."

Courtney scoffed inwardly. *No big deal?* That had to be at least two hundred photos. Since when had Angela been so generous with her time?

"One more thing." Jody held up a hand, then stepped back outside. Keeping the door blocked open, she hoisted in a box the size of a steamer trunk. "The league has invited a group of underprivileged girls from around Helena and they'd like to gift each of them with a Princess Pricilla doll."

Angela gave a dramatic toss of her head. "I hate those dolls. They never did get my nose right."

"Yes…well… It would be great publicity if you could sign each of the doll boxes." Jody waited, then added, "For the movie."

Courtney frowned at the box in an attempt to calculate how many dolls it must contain. At least fifty. Shouldn't she say something?

"All right." Angela shrugged nonchalantly.

"Wonderful." Jody released the breath she'd seemed to have been holding for the past few moments. "And if you could personalize each one, that would be just great."

"Mmm-hmm." Angela squinted into the mirror, giving the impression that she could no longer be considered an active participant in the conversation.

"I have a list of names." Jody held up a piece of paper and set it next to the photos. "I'll just leave it right here."

"Fine."

After lobbing Courtney an obligatory smile, Jody hurried out, as if afraid that Angela might renege if she didn't beat a hasty enough retreat.

With forced patience, Courtney watched as Angela sauntered over to the sofa. She sank deep into the cushions and crossed her long, bare legs. "Hand me my sandals, dear."

Glancing at the wealth of footwear that Angela had discarded around the room, Courtney reached for the pair nearest to her.

"Not *those*." Angela raised her twiglike arm and pointed. "The Manolo Blahniks."

Hoping to hurry along the process *and* avoid coming across like a total fashion ignoramus, Courtney crossed the room and picked up a pair of strappy brown leather flats that looked like they must have cost what to her would be a month's rent. Holding her breath, she offered them to Angela. Much to her relief, Angela took them without comment.

"I can't wait to get back to the house for a long, luxurious soak in the hot tub." Angela slid her foot into one of the shoes. "Doesn't that sound divine?"

Divine. Courtney frowned. *And time consuming.* Didn't Angela realize how long it would take to sign all those dolls and photos?

"I was almost nominated for a Golden Globe for *Princess Pricilla*. The kids will want to hear about that in my speech, don't you think?"

Her *speech?* This was a little fund-raiser, not the Academy Awards. Courtney fidgeted. If they left now, she could fit in at least two loads. Three if she ate while she sorted.

"It's important to be humble, don't you agree?" Angela bent down to buckle her other shoe. "So don't make me sound too braggy."

Courtney's eyes popped wide open. Angela expected *her* to write this speech? So now she was Ben Stein? She bit her lower lip. *Fine.* She could crank out a soliloquy during the spin cycle.

"Is my car waiting?" Angela stood and smoothed the front of her dress.

Finally. "Yes. It's right outside." Courtney grabbed the stack of photos and gauged if the box of dolls would fit into the trunk of the Town Car.

Angela arched an eyebrow. "Don't you think you should stay here? You want to do a good job on that speech, and there's so much distraction at the house."

Distraction? Courtney gave her a dumb stare. *Like that mountain of laundry?*

"Besides, you wouldn't want to have to haul that box around." Angela brushed a hand toward the dolls. "You can just sign them here. Same with the photos."

Seriously? Angela expected her to write a speech *and* forge her autograph? Wasn't that last part actually illegal?

"Ciao, *bella*." Angela waggled the fingers of one hand and disappeared out the door.

"But…" Courtney's voice trailed off as her new plan for the evening sank in. So much for clean clothes and a full stomach.

Courtney shook out her hand, unable to discern if its numbness came from low blood sugar or from carefully copying Angela's autograph for the past hour. Probably both.

A growl in her belly reminded her not only that she had missed dinner, but that lunch had been a Clif Bar while en route from Angela's dressing room to the wardrobe trailer on a quest for the perfect insoles.

As she glanced at her watch, her stomach clenched for a different reason. Adrenaline propelled her to the sofa, and she yanked back the curtain from the open window. She breathed out relief at the sight of the crew bus still parked up the drive. If she missed that, she'd be stuck at the ranch for the night, and then what? It wasn't like she could crash in the bed meant for Angela to rest on between takes.

She giggled at the thought, shifting her weight from one knee to the other. This *sofa* was pretty cushy. Maybe getting stranded here for the night wouldn't be so terrible.

None of her clothes at the house were clean anyway, so what would be the big deal? She chuckled. Of course, she could always borrow the Nicole Miller. *Right.* Like *that* wouldn't get her fired.

Relishing her unplanned but well-earned break, she gazed at the distant mountains. The sky had softened into its evening colors and the heat of the day dissolved to a comfortable coolness. For the first time, she could see the ranch not as a bustling movie set, but as a serene utopia. A smile coaxed the corners of her lips. How much of this peacefulness could she attribute to Angela's not being there?

A movement by the barn caught her attention, sending her nerves into a flutter. *Adam.* The poor guy was finally hammering on his fence. The smile she'd been restraining grew as she cupped her chin in her hands and stopped caring about her unfinished work. Right now, she was just a girl sneaking a peek at a hunky, and completely off-limits, guy.

Just then, a girl Courtney didn't recognize rode from behind the barn on a horse that looked an awful lot like Miss Molly. Courtney leaned in. It *was* Miss Molly, she was sure of it.

Adam stood, patted Miss Molly's nose and said something to the girl. The trill of her chipper response lilted through the evening air, and Courtney frowned. What was this feeling? Jealousy? *No way.* But something annoyingly close to it.

That was dumb. What did it matter if Adam talked to a cute—Courtney squinted to get a closer look—yes, *cute* girl? She slumped lower into the couch. It was none of her business.

Hold on. She straightened. If some girl caught Adam's eye, wouldn't that make it harder for Courtney to get him to spend time with Angela? And knowing Angela, she wouldn't take kindly to sharing his attention. In fact, she'd probably blame Courtney for not keeping better tabs on him. Her emotions thumped audibly in her chest. Maybe this *was* her business.

She leaped to her feet and paced a few steps back and forth. Nothing in her training had prepared her for this aspect of the job. Too bad Disappearing the Diva's Competition 101 hadn't been a college requirement.

There had to be a way to put a stop to this. She propelled herself back to the window and drilled her eyes into the girl who, as if reading her thoughts, steered Miss Molly away from Adam and started to trot her around the yard. Giving her a good-natured shake of his head, Adam moved toward the barn. That was good. Courtney could talk to him alone and get him to commit to giving Angela riding lessons, but she'd have to act fast. She squared her shoulders and charged out the door.

Moving briskly toward the barn as Adam disappeared inside, her confidence rose. She wasn't about to let a perky little cowgirl stand between her and a job well done.

Just as her hand touched the metal handle of the rough wooden barn door, a thumping noise made her stop short. She yanked back her hand. *That couldn't be...could it?* She stepped around a stack of hay bales, peering past the corner of the barn just in time to see Adam gallop away, dust puffing under Rocky's hooves.

Her heart thumped against her ribs. She had to call him back! Without thinking, she pulled in a deep breath, but the pungent odor of livestock launched her into a humiliating coughing fit. Through watery eyes, she watched as Adam and Rocky disappeared behind a bluff.

She stumbled around the hay in a feeble attempt to follow him. Was she crazy? As if she'd have any idea which way to go after she rounded that bluff. It wasn't as if she had a "back forty" app on her phone.

"Hey, are you okay?" A female voice called out from some distance behind her.

Courtney turned as the cute cowgirl swung down from Miss Molly. *Great.* It wasn't enough that she kept making a fool of herself. Did there always have to be witnesses?

"I—I'm fine." Courtney managed to call out in spite of the barnyard dust clogging her throat. "Really."

"You're Courtney." The girl vaulted easily over the corral fence, then made a self-conscious face. "Like you didn't know that."

Courtney squinted. Even through her cough-induced blurriness, it was clear that the girl was younger—and far less threatening—than she'd appeared from a distance. Courtney breathed a little easier.

"I'm Janessa." The girl bounced up to her, like a cheer-leader minus the pom-poms. "I'm guessing you wanted Adam?"

"I…uh…." Courtney felt a little silly, seeing now that the catalyst for her urgency was barely more than a kid. Maybe her talk with Adam could wait until tomorrow after all. "It's not that important."

"Oh." Janessa laced her fingers together as if she wasn't sure what to do with her hands. "He went to check on the fellas he has working on a drainage problem. No telling how long he might be."

"I see." Courtney bit her lip to keep from spitting out the dust in her mouth. "Well, I should get back to work then. I've got a project to finish before tomorrow, and—"

"For Angela Bijou?" A hopeful smile lit up Janessa's creamy-smooth face. "Can I help? I mean…if you need it."

Courtney held up a hand and took a step backward. There was no way she could supervise a high school girl to do this job, and if Angela found out, she'd have her head. "Thanks, but—"

The sound of the crew bus roaring to life cut her off. She whirled around to see a group of lighting guys walking to-ward it.

"Oh, snap." Her stomach roiled. "I have to run and grab my stuff from the dressing room and catch this bus. If they leave without me, I'm stuck." She started toward Angela's trailer.

"Well, let me help you with *that* then." Janessa caught up with her.

With no time to argue, Courtney picked up her pace. A couple other guys were headed for the bus now, too, and she had about five minutes, tops.

"You're so lucky. Andra and I—she's my best friend—we

love Angela Bijou." Janessa's cheerful chatter would have been endearing under less stressful circumstances. "You have the best job in the world."

"I guess so. It's not as exciting as it sounds."

"Hey, it's gotta be more exciting than living here. All I ever do besides work is ride my horse and do chores."

Realization dawned. "So, you live here then?"

"I grew up on the ranch." She tilted her a grin. "It's not as exciting as it sounds."

Courtney returned a quick smile.

Janessa continued to chatter. "I'd rather live in a city any day. That's what I'm saving up for. To move to Seattle."

Tossing her a befuddled glance, Courtney reached for the door to the trailer. This place was so peaceful and perfect. Why did Janessa want to leave?

Courtney darted inside and scanned the room for her backpack. Seeing it on the floor next to the sofa, she scoffed. No way would all those photos fit in there.

"Oh, my gosh. This is really her dressing room?" Janessa stood in the doorway, taking in the room.

"Yeah. Hey, do you want to help me carry this box?"

"Sure!" Edging forward to grab one side of the doll box, Janessa crinkled her brow. "What is this?"

Courtney scooped up the unsigned photos with one arm, and attempted to push her side of the box with the other. "Dolls. Princess Pricilla dolls I have to stay up half the night to sign."

"*You* have to?" Janessa wrapped her arm around the back of the box and started to push. "But shouldn't Angela Bijou be the one to—"

"Not in the real world." Shifting her grip on the photos, Courtney attempted to push her side of the box with both hands. Suddenly, all the photos slipped from her grasp and fanned across the floor in a pathetic display of fatigue and poor judgment. She let out a frustrated yowl and dropped to her knees.

"I'm always doing stuff like that. Clumsy." Janessa stooped down beside her. "Not you. Me, I meant."

Scrambling to collect the photos, Courtney tried to remain calm. That was probably what she got for venting her job frustrations to an innocent stranger.

Just then, the sound of the bus shifted from a rumble to a roar. "No!" She heaved herself to her feet in time to see it lumbering down the drive, then ran to the door of the trailer as if there were anything she could do to will it back. She should have asked the driver to wait for her.

She flapped her hands at shoulder level. "This can't happen."

"What's the matter?"

"That was the last bus. The one that waits for the stragglers. I can't believe they didn't check to make sure…" What was she thinking? They would have assumed she'd left with Angela hours ago in her car. This was all her fault.

"Well, if a ride is all you need—" Janessa joined her in the doorway "—Adam can take you back to town."

Adam. Why did her heart involuntarily pitch at the sound of his name?

"In fact, you could stay for dinner, and then I can help you finish your work. Adam won't mind waiting."

She winced. Was Adam used to being treated like the hired help? Then again, he *was* the hired help. Maybe he really *wouldn't* mind. Besides, that would give her plenty of time to talk him into giving Angela riding lessons. Still, he probably had to get up early and she shouldn't make him wait up just to take her home.

"Thanks, but—"

"We're having roast beef." Janessa's tone taunted. "It's Tuesday night, so the cook stays. I cook on weekends, but Tandy is way better than me."

Roast beef? Her stomach rumbled. That pretty much clinched it. "Okay. I'd love to stay."

"Great!" Victory filled Janessa's face like she'd scored a winning goal. "I'm so psyched about getting to know you better."

As they stepped outside, Courtney pondered. It wasn't like she was the movie star here. Why would Janessa want to get to know *her* better?

Chapter 11

The savory aroma of roast beef nestled in Courtney's nose as Janessa led her into the foyer of the house. She caught her breath, her gaze spanning the spacious front room.

"This is it." Janessa sounded almost apologetic as she shut the carved oak door behind them. "Home sweet home."

"Sweet is right." Courtney had to tip her head back to take in the high ceiling and what looked like an authentic gas-lit, crystal chandelier at its midpoint. "This room is incredible."

A hand-knotted rug, centered on the polished-wood floor, seemed too beautiful to walk on, so she stopped at its edge. A staircase gracefully curved up the wall to her right, conjuring up a muddled image of Scarlett O'Hara linking arms with Leo DiCaprio.

Impressive. She had been on some elaborately decorated film sets, but the historical detail in this room put them all to shame. "The swing gang must have gone into overtime getting your house ready for the movie."

Janessa's forehead puckered. "The *what* gang?"

Courtney gave a light laugh. "Sorry. Movie lingo. They're the part of the preproduction crew that came out to fix up the rooms we're using. They made your house shine like something out of *Better Homes and Heirlooms.*"

"Thanks—I think." Janessa moved next to her. "But they didn't have to do a whole lot. This room hasn't changed in like a hundred and thirty years. My family isn't big on redecorating."

"Seriously?" Courtney surveyed the room with bolstered admiration.

Janessa sighed. "I can't believe I get to be an extra in a movie with Angela Bijou and Jeffrey Mark Caulfield. In my own backyard." She let out a little squeal. "God is so good!"

Courtney squinted her a look, surprised by the unapologetic declaration of faith. It had been a long time since she'd been around folks who habitually gave God credit for anything. She'd grown used to being in the company of people who grabbed whatever glory they could for themselves as a flagrant display of self-promotion.

"Come on." Janessa inclined her head toward an arched doorway. "The dining room's this way, and I can totally smell Tandy's homemade biscuits."

Courtney followed her into a warm, inviting room that was painted a deep sage and accented by high windows draped in rich brown velvet. A set of double sliding doors flanked one wall, and an ornate dark-wood hearth invited her to cozy up on one of the brocade settees in front of it and call it a day.

"People who live in the twenty-first century would call this a family room but we call it the parlor."

"'Parlor' sounds so much more refined." Curious, Courtney shifted closer to a wall dotted with elegantly framed sepia photos. One of a little girl on a horse caught her attention. "Is that you?"

Janessa wrinkled her nose. "Yeah. I must have been about eight."

Courtney perused the arrangement of happy family photos. There was one of tiny Janessa on horseback with a cute dark haired boy. She pointed to the photo. "Hey, do you have a bro…"

She held her thought as the double doors glided open, revealing an elegant middle-aged woman and an opulent Victorian dining room behind her.

"I thought I heard voices in here." The woman moved gracefully into the room and gave Janessa a sideways hug. Her warm gaze landed on Courtney.

"Mama, this is Courtney." Janessa held up a hand. "She's Angela Bijou's personal assistant. Isn't that sick?"

"Sick? Is that a good thing?" The woman reached out a delicately manicured hand. "It's so nice to meet you, Courtney. Will you stay for dinner?"

Courtney shook her hand. "I'd love to. You have a beautiful home."

"Why, thank you. I can't take much credit. It's been in the family for over a century, and I only married into it a few decades ago."

"But it's filled with your warmth and spirit, and you should take full credit for that."

Courtney swallowed a gasp as Travis Bloom entered from the dining room.

"Mr. Bloom." Janessa's cheeks lost color as she glanced from him to her mother and back again. "Why are *you* here?"

Courtney flinched at the slight edge to Janessa's tone. Didn't she know that Travis Bloom was one of the most successful directors ever? One Travis Bloom in her parlor was worth twelve Angela Bijous in her backyard.

"Why, Janessa, he's our guest for dinner." Her mother placed a hand on Mr. Bloom's arm as he moved to her side with obvious affection, sliding a subtle hand to her lower back.

Suddenly, his presence at the ranch was less of a mystery.

"Travis, I'd like you to meet Courtney. She's a friend of Janessa's."

"Ms. Jacobs." He extended his other hand, sending Courtney's pulse into hyperdrive. "I'm so pleased to see you again." He spoke to Janessa's mother. "We met while the kids were out riding."

He remembered her! Of all the directors in Hollywood, Travis Bloom would be her first choice to work with, and here she was about to have dinner with him. Why didn't she have a résumé with her?

"Well, Tandy's ready to serve." Janessa's mother glanced toward the foyer as if hopeful that someone else would materialize. "I suppose we might as well start." Returning to the sumptuous dining room, she indicated a chair next to the head of the table. "Courtney, you can sit there."

Entering the room, Courtney admired the beautiful place settings, fascinated that the entire table had been set as if they'd expected company.

Just as she was about to reach for her chair, Adam burst into the room through a door on the adjacent wall, practically charging right into her. Her breathing all but stopped. They stared at each other, Adam apparently as startled as she was.

"About time," Janessa tossed off with a teasing tone as she crossed behind Adam and took the chair opposite Courtney.

"Oh, good." Janessa's mother moved to the far side of the table, where Mr. Bloom hurried to pull out her chair. "Courtney, have you met my son, Adam?"

Her son? Courtney's jaw practically clunked into her clavicle. But that would make him—

"Courtney and I have met, Mama." Bemusement flitted across his face as he moved Courtney's chair back and looked at her expectantly.

Lightheadedness threatened. His family *owned* this ranch. How could she have thought he was just a working-class guy with nothing better to do than cater to the whims of a spoiled actress?

"Excellent." Janessa's mother...*Adam's* mother (would that make her Mrs. Greene?) looked pleased. "I'm so glad you're here, dear. I was worried that you'd miss dinner again."

Courtney smiled wanly. He was staying for dinner. Of course he was—he lived here. Now not only was she faced with her one shot at making a good impression on her hoped-for future employer, but she'd be doing it in the presence of a guy who had currently robbed her of all ability to form a complete sentence. Suddenly, her belly started up some kind of Cirque du Soleil aerobatic act that made the prospect of taking in food seem unwise.

"Now, Mama, how could I miss roast beef night?" Adam inclined his temple toward the chair he still held out for Courtney, and she sat, her pulse spiking at his nearness.

"I've always said that on a ranch the best way to lure the men away from their work is with the smell of a good meal." Mrs. Greene spread a napkin across her lap.

"The same is true on a movie set." Mr. Bloom added.

As Adam sat next to Courtney at the table's head, their eyes locked for a second or two. She felt a sudden camaraderie with all the ladies contemporary to this room who had swooned due to a too-tight corset.

"I'm sure your movie crew is no different than our ranch hands." Mrs. Greene seemed oblivious to the dynamic going on at the other end of the table.

As Courtney tried to concentrate on the conversation, Adam's proximity to her, coupled with the sideways glances she felt from Janessa on his other side, made it impossible not to look at him.

"You're here," she said softly. Could she have uttered a less intelligent observation?

"I was about to say something along those same lines." He

kept his voice low, just for her to hear. "I thought you were gone for the night."

"Oh. N-no." It didn't go unnoticed that he had thought enough about her to assume she'd left for the day. Of course, that didn't mean anything. She scooted her chair a little closer. Did it?

Just then, a largish woman in a flour-speckled apron entered carrying a platter of sliced roast beef and set it down in front of Adam.

"That smells great, Tandy. Thank you." He gave her a nod and an appreciative smile.

Courtney saw him with fresh eyes. He was a businessman with responsibilities. Guilt and shame welled in her throat. Who was she to tamper with his emotions, allowing Angela to use him like just another chorus boy?

"And don't you even think of stealing away our Tandy for one of your catering crews." Mrs. Greene joked to Mr. Bloom, then turned to Adam. "Would you lead us in grace, dear?"

Adam extended one hand toward Courtney and the other toward Janessa. Courtney took in a sharp breath. The idea of fitting her hand into his gave her a sudden bolt of confusion. Their eyes met for a brief moment and he slipped her an almost imperceptible wink before sliding his fingers around hers. He bowed his head and gave a little cough.

Courtney's heartbeat went into some kind of overdrive. It was like that time George Clooney had touched her arm, except really nothing like that at all. George Clooney was a handsome movie star, but Adam was—

"Heavenly Father."

His robust baritone pulled Courtney from her thoughts, and she snapped her eyes shut.

"Thank You for providing this meal."

His work-roughened hand held hers with an assuredness that she didn't quite know what to make of. Could he feel the adrenaline surging to her fingertips?

"That we can enjoy the company of our dinner guests and that the problems of the day have been handled with as much grace as we could muster."

Electricity surged up Courtney's arm, and it was all she could do not to yelp. He had to have felt that, but his voice remained calm and steady. It must just be her low blood sugar again.

"And most of all thank You, Lord, for Your grace and Your bountiful blessings."

He gave her hand a tiny squeeze before letting go—or had she just imagined it? She opened her eyes and glanced in his direction.

He appeared totally at ease as he spread his napkin across his lap and looked around the table. When their eyes met, he smiled politely and reached for a slice of roast beef, offering it to her.

Her heart skipped. She didn't want Angela to hurt him, but why was she doing this to herself? Was she really so juvenile as to be going gaga over a handsome cowboy? Who clearly, she had to admit, wasn't having the same reaction to her.

She fastened her gaze firmly on the bowl of mashed potatoes Mr. Bloom passed her way and lifted a hefty scoop onto her plate. Of course Adam wasn't interested in her. What was she thinking? She was only there to make a movie, after all, then she'd be going home. It made no sense that she felt disappointed in his lack of interest.

But what if…?

She tried to keep her eyes off him, but failed. What if she weren't there *temporarily…?*

Biting her lower lip, she took a healthy helping of carrots. If he hadn't been sitting next to her at the table, so obviously flesh and blood and real, she could have sworn he came straight out of a movie script. A muscular cowboy who was as at home on a horse as he was in a formal dining room. An honest man of strong faith, funny and nice-looking and—

Whoa. What was she thinking? She was there to work, not to crush on some guy. She didn't have time for this. She took a bite of a biscuit but didn't taste it. Besides, it apparently hadn't deterred Adam that *Angela* was only there temporarily. He'd seemed anxious enough to involve himself with her on a fleeting basis.

She let out a breath. Why was she even comparing herself to a glamorous, wealthy movie star? Of course he wouldn't pass up the opportunity to dally with Angela. What man would?

If she hadn't been afraid of her own poor aim, she would have kicked herself. She was having dinner with Travis Bloom, and letting Adam totally distract her from this awesome career opportunity. Forget ogling. This was the time for networking.

"Mr. Bloom." She revolved boldly to her right. "Tell us about your next project."

"I'm glad you asked." He swallowed a bite of food, then continued. "It's a moving story of a woman who smuggles Bibles into China."

"Oh?" She cut off a small piece of roast beef. "What's it called?"

"Unofficially, it's being pitched around town as 'The Travis Bloom Project'—not my idea, by the way." He gave Courtney a knowing look. "As I'm sure you're aware, at this point it's all about getting names attached to it to attract interest, and apparently my name appeals to some people."

As a round of chuckles circled the table, Courtney congratulated herself. Mr. Bloom had acknowledged her as a movie insider, who clearly understood the minute dynamics of the process. Smiling, she took a delicate bite of her carrots so that eating wouldn't impede her ability to keep talking. She was on a roll.

"It sounds interesting." She swallowed. "Will you be filming in China?"

"China and several other locations."

"Good." Janessa swirled her gravy with her fork. "Then you won't have any business in Montana for a while."

"Janessa!" Her mother pinned her with a sharp glare.

Janessa shrank back. "Mama, I'm just saying."

"It's true." Mr. Bloom seemed to overlook her teenagerly rudeness. "Once we begin shooting, I'll be globe-hopping for several months, but I do anticipate a nice long rest after we wrap." He gave Mrs. Greene a fond look that spoke volumes.

"Well," Courtney confidently continued, "I personally love traveling for work. It's one of my favorite parts of the job."

A quick glance at Adam said that she was a jet-setter just like Angela. On the move with better things to do than to pine away for some guy who was only interested in a short-term romance with a hot actress.

"You've got quite the assignment on this one, I understand." Mr. Bloom popped the last of a biscuit into his mouth. "How are you faring as Angela's assistant?"

"Oh, great." How could she emphasize her competency without sounding like she was bragging? "It's a dream job. She's just wonderful to work for."

"She is?" Janessa's brow creased. "She doesn't seem like it to me."

"Why would you say that, Janessa?" Polishing off his roast beef, Mr. Bloom appeared sincerely interested.

Courtney jumped in. "She just means—"

"It doesn't seem very 'wonderful' of her to expect you to stay up half the night tonight doing her work." Janessa shrugged a shoulder in innocent observation.

"Her work?" Mr. Bloom turned a questioning look to Courtney. "Don't tell me she expects you to memorize her lines for her."

"No, nothing like that. It's just some dolls and photos I have to get ready for a personal appearance she has in the morning." Courtney shot a warning glance at Janessa. "That's all."

Mr. Bloom seemed to consider her response. *Terrific.* Now he probably thought she was an ungrateful employee.

Peripherally, she sensed Adam studying her. Just what she needed—everyone judging her ability to perform her job.

Just then Tandy entered the room with a couple of pies, which she set on the sideboard.

"Tandy," Mrs. Greene said. "When we're done here, Mr. Bloom and I will have our dessert and coffee out on the porch."

"Of course, Mrs. Greene."

Adam sopped up the gravy on his plate with a biscuit. "Just leave the other pie, Tandy. The girls and I will take it with us. And I think we'll need some coffee in one of those big carafes."

"Oh, and Tandy." Mrs. Greene spoke again. "Mr. Bloom will be coming for lunch tomorrow, so if you wouldn't mind making us some sandwiches with the leftover roast, that would be fine."

Tandy nodded and returned to the kitchen.

Courtney slowly chewed, eyeing Adam and awaiting an explanation. Where exactly were they going?

He looked her way and smiled lightly. In the same moment he swallowed, Janessa apparently kicked him, because he jumped and looked at her. "Ow! What was that for?"

She rolled her eyes. "Courtney wants to know where we're going with pie and coffee, Bozo."

He put down his fork and looked at Courtney. "Isn't it obvious?"

Her eyes narrowed, begging him to continue.

"To Miss Bijou's trailer. We have work to do."

"*We* do?" Panic welled. This was all she needed—for Adam to imply that she couldn't handle her workload. "But… it's not really something that…I mean, I can't ask you to—"

"So what happens if it doesn't get done?" Adam raised an eyebrow.

"I don't know." She fished for a save. "I'll never work in this town again?"

Mr. Bloom chuckled, thank goodness.

Adam topped his plate with his napkin. "That's what I thought. Now we'd best get a move on."

Chapter 12

Adam sat on the floor of Angela's trailer, leaning against the sofa and shaking his head at Janessa and Courtney as they reached the tail end of a giggling fit.

"You should have seen Adam run!" Janessa had spent more time spinning yarns about him as a kid than she had signing boxes, but that was fine by Adam. She'd kept them entertained and had functioned as an unwitting chaperone.

"Yeah, I ran all right." He lifted his black pen and examined the photo he had just signed. "But only because you were screaming like a banshee." He grabbed the last photo and signed it, doing his best to keep it away from what remained of the huckleberry pie that sat in the middle of the coffee table.

"I can totally picture it." Still tittering, Courtney grabbed her plate and reclined next to him. "This pie is fabulous. I could so get used to the way you eat out here."

"It helps to have the best cook this side of the Rockies working for us." Adam arched a brow at his sister. "Too bad we have to starve on the weekends."

Janessa grabbed a pillow from the chair behind her and tossed it at his head. "Whatever, Adam."

"Kidding." Adam raised his hands to fend off the fluffy projectile. "I'm kidding. You're an awesome cook, Ness."

Janessa looked at Courtney. "You see what I have to put up with?"

Courtney giggled as she ran her fork over what remained of the crumbs on her plate. "I get it, believe me. I have a brother myself."

Looking from the coffee table full of signed photos to Courtney and then Adam, Janessa raised her arms in a huge stretch and made a big show of patting her mouth in a bogus yawn. "Boy, oh boy. I can hardly keep my eyes open."

Adam tipped her a smirk. "Subtle, Janessa."

She squinted at him and stood, giving Courtney a warm grin. "Good night, Courtney. Have fun at that movie thing tomorrow."

"I will now that I'll be able to get some sleep beforehand. And I never would have written such an inspired speech by myself. Thanks for all your help."

"No prob." She started for the door. "Big bro and I live to serve."

With that, Janessa disappeared out the door, and Courtney set down her pie plate and surveyed the stack of photos in front of them. "We're done? I can't believe we actually did it."

"Yep." He glanced at his watch. "It's late, and I think tomorrow's going to come too soon for both of us." He pulled himself to his feet, then offered her a hand up. "Now, let's get this box into the truck so it can travel with you in the morning."

The warmth of her fingers sent an unexpected lightning bolt up his arm and straight to his heart. Did she feel it, too?

She let go a little more quickly than he would have liked. "Sounds good."

"Where do they have you staying?" He grabbed the box and she picked up the photos. "The Elkhorn Inn?"

"That's for the crew." She mimicked a look down her nose. "The company rented a private home for Ms. Bijou. Some rich family's so-called cabin, just south of town."

He nodded. "Yeah, most of those cabins are worth a couple mil at least."

"This one is, that's for sure. I'm lucky to get to stay there with her. It's one of the perks of my job."

Stepping outside, Adam breathed in the crisp air, enjoying the moment and trying not to think too far ahead.

Courtney walked alongside him. "I'm curious about something."

Looking down at her, he huffed with exertion. "What's that?"

"Is your mom the reason Mr. Bloom is in Montana?"

"Mama?" His brow pinched in confusion. "What are you talking about?"

She gave him one of those looks that women frequently give men when they think they're being thickheaded. "He obviously has his eye on her."

"What?" That couldn't be...*could* it?

"Oh, come on, you had to have noticed. Isn't that why Janessa is so down on him?"

A dull pain settled in his chest. "That's not why she's down on him."

"Oh. Well, then why?"

Hoisting the dolls into the back of his truck, he let out a sigh. "She's down on him because she doesn't want me to sell him our ranch."

Her weary eyes opened wide. "What? Why would you sell your ranch?"

He moved to her side of the truck and opened the door for her. "It's complicated."

As he crossed around to his own door, a debate swirled

in his tired brain. How much should he share with her? He climbed into the truck and started the engine, feeling her eyes on him as she waited for an answer.

"The economy's been so bad the past couple of years." Putting his arm on the seat back, he maneuvered the truck into a three-point turn. "It's not just the ranch. It's the whole town."

"The town's in trouble? But it's so cute. It would make a great little tourist destination."

"Maybe." He sighed. "Folks have been real grateful for the money the movie company has brought to our community, but with the ranchers not making much profit, everyone suffers."

"Oh…." Her voice trailed off.

He went on, buoyed by her concern. "Anyway, the Bar-G got really behind financially. I kept thinking things would turn around, like they always do." Shifting into Drive, he looked toward the main road. "Lately, things have improved, but I'm afraid it's too bad to save without some kind of miracle."

"So—" concern tinted her tone "—you basically just need a chunk of money to put you back in the black?"

"Yeah. But I just don't see how that's going to happen." The truck rumbled onto the vacant highway. "I've been praying…the whole family has."

"So, how did Mr. Bloom enter the picture?"

"Well, a lot of wealthy people buy property in Montana. I guess they see it as a great retreat from their high-stress world. Apparently he was looking for a ranch and word got out that we might be in a good position to sell. He drove up one day and made me a very generous offer."

"Whoa. It must be hard to say no. People like him tend to get what they want."

"Well, he knows we're strapped for money. He's the one who suggested to Keith Kingsley that he should send the location scouts out to our place to consider it for the movie."

"That pays really well." Her voice brightened. "It must have helped."

"It helped a lot, but not enough. So, I'm still considering Mr. Bloom's proposition. I have to think maybe it was God's answer to prayer."

"Hmm." She twisted toward him in her seat. "Say you do sell the ranch. Would you stay in Thornton Springs?"

A corner of his mouth twitched. Was that hope in her voice? "Mr. Bloom has kindly offered me the job of ranch foreman, which means I'd move into the foreman's house with Leonard and draw a paycheck. Be kind of a relief, truth be told."

"Oh." She shifted forward. "And your family?"

"Janessa's moving to Seattle soon as she saves up the money, and Mama says the house is too big for just the two of us. She says she wants to buy herself a little place in town."

"Sounds like a plan."

"It's a plan, all right. There's only one thing wrong with it."

"What's that?"

Uneasiness churned in his gut. Did he really want to tell her this? He swallowed hard. "It's just that I always dreamed of raising a family of my own there."

From the corner of his eye, he saw her look his way, but she didn't respond.

"I know it sounds crazy." He gazed at the moonlit mountains that rose up ahead of them. "But I've had this image of someday teaching my own kids everything my dad taught me and his dad taught him." Why was it suddenly difficult to swallow? "Passing the ranch down to my own kids seems like an important part of that."

"That doesn't sound crazy to me." Her voice sounded soft, sweet.

"Unrealistic, then." He sighed. "I don't know. Maybe I'm just having a hard time letting go of something that's not meant to be."

Silence stretched. Courtney seemed to be considering what he'd just said.

"But you want to know the worst part?" He turned onto the main street of town, which was dark and quiet at this time of night. "Makes me feel like a failure."

"A failure?" She faced him again. "Adam, the whole country's having financial difficulties right now."

"Sure, but generations of Greene men have had difficulties. Wars. The Great Depression. They never lost the ranch, and now I feel like I'm failing the family."

A deep exhale came from her side of the cab, and Adam detected her listing subtly toward him. He never talked to anybody about this, but telling Courtney had been surprisingly easy.

She wrapped her arms around herself, relaxing. "Your dad…he's…"

"Been gone for about ten years now." It still stung to talk about it. That's why he normally didn't.

"I'm so sorry." She paused. "I can't even think about what life would be like without one of my parents."

He snagged the opportunity to change the subject. "They live in Fresno?"

She looked at him, a slight smile playing on her lips. "You remembered. Yeah, they're still there. I don't see them much. They're so active with their church, now that my brother Ben and I are gone."

He perked up. This was the first mention she'd made of church. He'd sensed that she had that quality that comes with faith in the Lord, but he hadn't known for sure. "So…what church do they attend?"

"Christ Faith. It's the church I grew up in."

"So you're a Christian?"

"Yes. I mean I was. Go left up there." She pointed to a turnoff. "Now I don't really know."

His heart dipped as he turned the wheel. Maybe this was

his confirmation that he shouldn't think of Courtney as anything more than a friend. On the other hand, maybe God was at work here. Maybe He wanted Adam to draw Courtney back to her faith.

"What are you unsure about?"

"Church used to be really important to me. But then I went to college, and the people at my new church seemed so judgmental. Maybe I used that as an excuse to drift away and do my own thing, I don't know. But now I'm totally caught up in my career, and I'll tell you one thing—there's no place for God in Hollywood."

One side of Adam's mouth quirked. "So you got into the movie business and you lost your faith."

"It's not so much that I *lost* it. I—"

"You lost your faith."

"I guess." Her voice grew quiet. "I guess maybe I did."

"And here you are."

"Here I am…?"

"You do know that God works in mysterious ways."

"So I've heard. What's that got to do with me?"

"You went to college and lost your faith. Maybe you came to Montana to get it back."

She took in a breath as though she wanted to respond, but no words came. They drove in silence for a moment or two.

"Turn right here." Her voice sounded low, contemplative. "It's just up this long drive."

Adam's truck clunked its way up the steep incline, and he came to a stop in front of a four-car garage. The house attached to it stood tall and inviting, nestled in the trees. He killed the engine and leaned forward slightly to look up at the soaring triangle of front windows. A few lights were on, but all seemed still. "So…do you think Angela is awake?"

She eyed him for a second. "No. She's pretty big on getting her beauty sleep."

He nodded. *Good.* The last thing he wanted right now was

to have to wend his way through a flirtatious dialogue with Courtney's boss.

He got out of the car and crossed around the front, but by the time he reached the passenger's side, she had already gotten out.

A few moments later, inside the house, Adam set the box of dolls next to the front door.

"I'm parched." Courtney started for a doorway on the far side of the room. "Want some water before you start back?"

"Sure." He looked around the high-ceilinged room. It was a nice house—upscale but unpretentious.

Courtney returned, handed him a bottle of water—not *D'eau Douce,* he noted—and flung herself onto a plush sofa while she cracked open her own bottle. "I'm exhausted."

Opening his drink, he sat next to her, sinking back into the soft cushions. "You need a good night's sleep." He took a deep swig of the refreshing liquid, wondering how he was going to wake up in just a few hours himself.

She set her bottle on the table next to her and looked over at him. "Thanks again. For everything."

He wanted to say something, but what? This was one of those moments when he needed to guard his tongue. It would be so easy to say something that might lead them down the wrong road. He wasn't sure how she would react if he did— how she felt about him. The cautious approach seemed best. "If there's anything else I can do to make your job easier, just ask."

"Really?" Yawning, she closed her eyes. "Anything…?"

"Anything." He set his bottle on the table next to him. "Just ask." He waited for a response, but she didn't stir. "Court-ney…?"

"Hmm?" Her voice sounded dreamy and her breathing slow.

He bent toward her, wanting to push a wayward sandy-blond curl off her forehead, but resisting. "I have to go now.

Will I see you tomorrow?" He spoke softly, but she didn't respond.

What should he do…leave her there to sleep? Reluctantly, he stood and took a few careful steps toward the door.

"Adam?"

He turned, hesitating. Her eyes were shut and she looked more asleep than awake.

"Yes?"

"I want…" Her lids fluttered open slightly.

"What?" Cautiously, he treaded back and knelt next to her.

"I…" She seemed to be losing the fight to keep her eyes open. "I want…" Her voice fluttered barely above a whisper.

He drew closer. "What do you want?"

Eyes once again closed, her head rolled toward him. "…*you*…"

He reeled back. "What?"

Her eyes popped open, startled. "I mean *Angela*. Angela wants you…" she seemed flustered—tired—confused.

"Angela?"

"…to give her riding lessons." She sat up, putting her hands to her temples. "That's what I meant."

Confusion surged. "Riding lessons? Why?"

She sprang to her feet and started to pace, and he stood, too, trying to make sense of her words.

"She wants them to add a riding scene for her, and she insists that you should be the one who teaches her." She whirled around, looking a little frantic. "If I don't deliver what she wants, I'll look bad, and I might even get fired or at least never get hired again. I know you don't have time, but I really need you to say yes."

"Yes." He gripped her by the shoulders to calm her.

She stopped. Stared. "Really?"

Now that his hands were on her, he couldn't wrench them away. He rubbed her shoulders lightly, feeling the curve of her upper back through her sweat jacket. "I said I'd do anything you needed to help make your job easier."

"But…you said you didn't have time to—"

"I'll find the time." His eyes bored into hers.

She smiled shyly, looking like she wanted to say more. The smile said enough.

He grinned back, his heart a galloping steed, and she focused on his lips. He leaned in—

"Courtney!"

They both leaped backward at the sound of Angela's voice, putting a good five feet between them. Courtney folded her arms and Adam put a hand on his hip and rubbed the back of his neck.

"Do you think anyone delivers sushi at this time of night?" Angela slinked into the room wearing a filmy pink robe that did little to conceal a skimpy bikini underneath. "Remember I like extra wasabi." Her features sharpened when she saw Adam. "Well, hello, cowboy."

He cringed, avoiding looking at anything but her face. "Ma'am."

"I hope we didn't wake you." Courtney's voice quivered and she spoke a little too fast. "Adam just helped me bring these back for tomorrow." She pointed at the box, which had patiently bore witness to the events of the past several minutes.

"Wake me?" Angela slid toward him, flipping her wettipped hair over her shoulder. "I couldn't sleep, so I was relaxing in the hot tub." Her eyes locked on his. "Care to join me?"

"Oh, uh…no, thank you." He wanted to run, but that wouldn't do Courtney any good. "It's late, and…I'd best be heading home."

Angela shrugged. "Another time, then." Her eyes traveled to his feet and back up again. "When we *have* time." She did an about-face and waved a hand over her shoulder as she disappeared from the room.

Adam let out a low breath and looked at Courtney, who seemed to avoid his gaze. "I should go." He started for the door, and she followed.

He opened it, eased out onto the porch, then turned to face her in the doorway.

"Thanks again." Now her eyes met his, although she still appeared agitated.

He dipped a nod. "My pleasure, ma'am." That got her to smile.

He walked toward his truck, exhausted, confused and what? Elated?

Grabbing the handle to his truck door, he glanced over his shoulder at the house. *Oh, Lord, what next?*

Chapter 13

The woman from the Children's Welfare League practically fell over herself gushing to Angela as she escorted her and Courtney to the Town Car. "We just can't thank you enough, Ms. Bijou."

"Not a problem." Angela waved a slender hand. "It involved zero effort on my part."

Courtney choked down a chuckle. Angela was right—it *had* involved zero effort on her part. It felt a little wrong that the autographs weren't authentic, but at least the kids would never know the difference.

The driver moved to open the back door for Angela just as a man with a camera leaped out from behind the car. Angela made a disgusted noise and held up her hands in defense. He fired off several shots of her before the driver yanked him aside.

Seeing that the driver was occupied holding off the photog, Courtney finished the job of opening Angela's door.

"Pesky mosquitoes!" Angela dove into the car. "How on earth do they find me even in the middle of nowhere?"

Courtney pushed the door shut and smiled contritely at the Children's Welfare woman, whose mouth hung open in dismay.

"Ms. Bijou loved every minute of her time here." Courtney hoped she sounded convincing. "Thank you for inviting her."

The corners of the woman's mouth curved up in what looked like forced hospitality. Courtney hurried around the car and slid into the other side of the backseat as the driver got in and started the engine.

Angela's countenance had completely soured. "It's not enough that I have to put up with cameras in my face, but all that shrieking. Kids!" She took her compact out of her baby-pink Birkin bag and started to powder her nose. "And the parents. Ugh. If I see one more stroller, I'm going to scream. It's disgusting." She clicked the compact shut. "Where am I supposed to be today?"

Checking her clipboard, Courtney ran her finger down Angela's schedule. "Keith pushed the scene we were *going* to shoot today to tomorrow, to accommodate this morning's event. That means adding a day to the workweek to stay on course." Her lips rolled in as she awaited Angela's response to the news that they were now slated to work on Sunday. When she remained attentively silent, Courtney continued. "We're shooting the barn scene this afternoon, so you're due in makeup at twelve thirty."

"Fabulous. Call Travis Bloom and book an early lunch with him. Find someplace nice where I won't be bothered by the public. I can't stand to have people leering at me while I eat."

Courtney reached for her phone, then stopped. "Oh…I can't. I mean *he* can't."

"What do you mean?"

She gulped. "He's having lunch today at the Bar-G Ranch with the owner, Mrs. Greene."

"He is?" Angela's tone was one of deep affront. "How do *you* know?"

"Well, I—"

"It doesn't matter." She waved a hand. "He'll be happy to cancel for me." She leaned forward and tapped the driver on the shoulder. "Take us straight to the ranch. We'll head him off at the pass." She sat back, looking satisfied with herself. "I'm telling you, Courtney, Travis is a genius."

Courtney rolled her tense shoulders. Thinking of Mr. Bloom brought to mind her conversation with Adam, the memory of which she'd been dodging all morning. Then warm, if conflicted, thoughts followed. Talk about confused. She had made such a fool of herself when she'd almost fallen asleep and started babbling. At least he had said yes to teaching Angela, thank goodness. He'd been so sweet.

The tension worked its way down to her shoulder blades. Had he said "yes" to be nice to Courtney, or because he wanted to spend more time with Angela? After all, the horseback riding would be a perfect excuse for him to be alone with her.

"Did I tell you he wants me?" Angela tapped Courtney's arm.

Courtney's thoughts snapped back to the present. "What?"

"He wants me for the next project he's considering."

Courtney let out her breath. Angela was still talking about Mr. Bloom.

"It's a story about a woman who smuggles Bibles into China or India or someplace." Holding up her arm, she toyed with the diamond-encrusted bracelet dangling from her wrist. "It sounds perfect for me."

"China," Courtney said absentmindedly.

"What?"

"She smuggles Bibles into China."

Angela stared at her just long enough to make Courtney worry she'd have to explain how she knew this.

Giving a long blink, Angela lifted a shoulder. "Whatever. Anyway. Travis saw my last picture and he thinks I've grown as an actress. He compared me to Meryl Streep, can you believe it? Meryl Streep! She was my inspiration growing up."

Courtney half listened as she watched the scenery pass. Maybe Adam was right. Maybe she had lost her faith. Living her life for the Lord had been so important to her in high school, but now she had career aspirations. How could she possibly have both? Wouldn't that make her a hypocrite or something?

"Of course, it isn't surprising that people would make that comparison." Angela examined her nails. "I mean I'm told all the time that I inspire young people."

Courtney gave a halfhearted nod. The thought of someone having success in the movie business while walking a straight line with God intrigued her. Would that be possible for someone like *her?*

"Artistically speaking," Angela continued, "we only have so much in us and we have to be very careful what work we accept. I feel, and Travis agrees, that the message we send to the public is critical, especially in this day and age. We don't just want to entertain with our art, we want to inform and instruct."

Courtney allowed another thought about Adam. The Greene family seemed so…grounded. There was something so reassuring about being around them. They reminded her of her own family.

"I'm considering doing Broadway to enhance my credibility. What do you think?" Angela looked in Courtney's direction for a nanosecond. "Of course, with Broadway you don't reach as many people as with movies, so I don't know if it would be worth my time. I can't spread myself too thin, you know."

Tears started to choke Courtney. Her parents had asked her so many times if she was still reading her Bible and attending church. She had lied more than once, an edict broken so habitually in Hollywood it was practically expected.

"I always try to play women who can be good role models, especially to young people. Strong female characters need to be encouraged in modern cinema."

Courtney bobbed her head blandly. What if she did want God back at the center of her life? Was it too late? Sure, it was easy for someone like Adam to follow the Ten Commandments, but how could *she?* Most people in this industry broke at least three out of the ten before seeing the bottom of their first cup of morning coffee. It went with the territory.

"Of course, if I'm going to play strong characters, it's important that I actually be strong in my own life. That's why I make sure I refresh myself."

Courtney gave a desultory nod. That shouldn't stop her from at least praying once in a while. Maybe she could start reading her Bible again. She'd always gotten so much out of that. She knew there was no such thing as being a part-time Christian, but maybe she could find some sort of compromise.

"I wouldn't want to wear myself out. I've seen too many actresses make the mistake of working themselves to the point of exhaustion. You need some release…shopping…jetting off to Europe spontaneously. That sort of thing."

Biting her upper lip, Courtney smiled in superficial acknowledgment. Maybe it would be a good compromise to pray for other people. That would at least help her to not feel so selfish.

"You're never going to be any good for anybody else if you don't put yourself first all the time. I've learned that the hard way, believe me."

Courtney did her best to hear Angela while following through on her own thoughts. Adam had said that the town was in financial trouble, and that he had a big problem with the ranch. Maybe she should pray about that.

Closing her eyes, she tried to concentrate. *God, please*

put a big financial blessing on the people of this town. She paused, collecting her thoughts. *As for Adam, he's struggling right now to do the right thing. If it's Your will for him to keep the ranch and raise his own family there*—she tried to ignore the tingle in her tummy—*please show him the way. And, Lord, if You have anything in mind for the two of us besides friendship*—

Her eyes shot open. Where had *that* come from?

"Wait a minute." The accusation in Angela's voice tugged Courtney to attention. "You look strange. What were you just thinking about?" Angela focused on her with a searing intensity. "You know something, don't you?"

Panic welled in Courtney's chest. She'd have to deny any attraction to Adam. "I don't—"

"Yes, you do." Angela twisted in her seat to face her. "Why would Travis waste his time having lunch with that woman when he's clearly here to pursue me for his movie?"

Courtney nearly choked on her intended denial. So this wasn't about Adam. What was she supposed to do now? "He's discussing plans."

"Plans?" Suspicion arched in her brow. "What kind of plans?"

She shrugged one shoulder. "Something about buying the ranch."

Angela tittered. "Oh, is that all? Well, that makes sense then. He would *have* to wine and dine that woman if he wants to get a fair deal. Real estate is a game just like show business. It's all about negotiating and protecting one's own interests."

Courtney nodded. "I suppose."

"I'll just have lunch with the cowboy instead."

Courtney gasped. "Oh…uh…"

Angela slowly looked at her. "Is there a problem with that?"

A problem? She could give her a whole list. "It's just that… Adam might need to be in on the negotiations."

Angela made a big show of rolling her eyes. "That's ridiculous. It's not like it's any of his business if Travis buys a ranch."

Something about the dismissive, disrespectful tone in Angela's voice rubbed Courtney wrong. "It is his business, because it's his ranch."

Angela stared vacantly. "*His* ranch? But you just said that *woman* owns it." She gasped. "You're not saying that Adam's *married?*"

"Oh, no. Mrs. Greene is his mother."

"Oh." Angela looked ahead, her brow furrowing. "But it's a perfectly good ranch. Why on earth would they want to sell it?"

Courtney shrugged. She'd said way too much already. "It's expensive to run, I suppose."

"Yes…." The wheels in Angela's brain appeared to be grinding. "Not everyone has money…."

Courtney watched her, wishing she could read her mind.

Suddenly, Angela's expression reverted back to her usual self-absorbed calm. "I'm working too hard. I need to have some fun. Forget about arranging lunch. I can speak to Travis about that myself." She lifted her chin. "I want you to work a *real* date with Adam into my schedule. Take care of that soon."

A knot developed in Courtney's throat. She forced a smile and nodded, wondering exactly what it was that, in Angela's book, would make a date real. Was that God's answer to her prayer? Some great start to her Christian compromise.

She closed her eyes again. *Lord, Adam seems to really like Angela, and if it's in Your will for them to be together, please give me peace with that.*

With a heavy sigh, she watched as they curved into the drive for the ranch. She rolled in her lips. *Amen.*

Chapter 14

Stifling a yawn, Courtney leaned against the barn, waiting for the crew inside to finish prepping for the scene Angela and Jeffrey were about to shoot. It had been an agonizing afternoon, thanks to Angela's outrage over Mr. Bloom's gentle refusal to reschedule his lunch with Mrs. Greene. What did she expect? Courtney had secretly savored finally hearing someone say the word *no* to Angela, even though the resulting tsunami of indignation had largely come crashing down on *her*.

Now, in an attempt to regain her composure, Courtney relaxed her shoulders and allowed her senses to open to the beauty around her. The perfect clear sky, and the distant snow-dusted peaks eased the tension from her limbs. A dog barked in the distance, in soothing contrast to the hubbub inside the barn behind her.

A peripheral movement snagged her attention. Some distance away, in a fenced grassy pasture, Pepper trotted around Adam on the end of a long rope. Courtney's jaw clenched, and whatever composure she'd just gained slipped away. She hadn't seen him yet today, and still felt uncomfortable about last night.

Watching him work, sadness threatened. It had been so nice of him to cooperate with Angela's demands—whatever his personal motivation might be. She hated to think of him losing the ranch. She owed it to him to help, but how?

Revolving in a slow circle as Pepper pranced like a show horse, Adam tipped his hat forward to guard his eyes from the late-afternoon sun. His strong form seemed like such a part of this landscape. He should be able to have his dream… to raise a family here. It wasn't hard to see that he'd make a great dad someday.

A smile found her lips as she clasped her elbows and curved one leg to rest her dirt-encrusted boot against the barn. In her mind's eye, a child appeared on Pepper's back and she saw herself approaching with a picnic basket. She bit back a snicker. A picnic basket…and a baby. She pictured Adam taking the basket and setting it at their feet. He then took the baby and held him up, making him giggle. She looped an arm through Adam's and reached up to hold the small hand of the child on the horse. Adam looked at her. Their eyes met and he bent down—

"Does all this hay really have to be here? I think I'm allergic."

Angela's grating protest snapped Courtney back to reality, and her dream image disappeared like a cinematic special effect. Where had that come from, anyway? Becoming a wife and mother was a distant goal at best, and definitely not on a ranch. Why was she giving in to those thoughts about Adam?

She quickly entered the barn and crossed to Angela, countering Jeffrey, who rolled his eyes and muttered something unflattering about Angela under his breath.

Courtney forced a calm demeanor. "Can I get you anything, Ms. Bijou?"

"Yes, you can get *rid* of this hay. I simply cannot say my lines with all this dust in the air."

"You seem to be having no trouble talking *now*." Jeffrey fixed Angela with a glare that could have straightened a horseshoe.

Courtney inhaled. The smell of the barn had actually *grown* on her.

"Lose the hay!" The A.D.'s voice echoed inside the aged wooden structure and the place suddenly bustled with activity.

They had gotten a late start filming, thanks to the fundraiser. If they took the time to deal with this, they didn't stand a chance of wrapping the scene before they lost light.

"You!"

Courtney whipped around. Mr. Kingsley aimed his megaphone in her direction and charged toward her. Dread hit full force.

"Yes, sir?"

"Where's that cowboy who owns this place?" He snarled through gnashing teeth. "Find him and tell him he needs to convince Angela that we can't get rid of the hay."

"I'm on it." She hurried back outside, grateful that she knew Adam's whereabouts, but hating the idea of asking him one more favor.

As she rushed toward him, Adam cracked that tantalizing grin. The rope slackened, and Pepper ambled to Adam's side.

"Hey." He hooked a thumb in the front pocket of his jeans. "How'd the dolls go over?"

"Great. The kids loved them." Standing in the very spot where she had nearly kissed him in her daydream, a blush crept up her neck.

"How's it going in there?" He tilted his chin toward the barn, skepticism creasing his brow.

Turning away slightly so he wouldn't notice her cheeks transforming into two ripe tomatoes, she stroked Pepper's dusty, velvety muzzle. "Well, I have good news and bad news."

An agreeable smile flashed beneath his *what-now* frown.

The soft fuzz of Pepper's lips nuzzling her hand prompted a titter. "The bad news is Angela thinks she's allergic to hay."

He huffed out an ironic chuckle.

"But the good news is that Mr. Kingsley thinks you're the man to tell her the hay has to stay in the barn."

Tilting back his hat, he tossed her a bemused frown. "And why is that *good* news?"

Good question. "Because…" She didn't want to point out the obvious—it was an opportunity for him to talk to Angela. "You get a chance to swoop in and be the hero to the entire crew."

"Uh-huh." Amusement creased his eyes. "Nice try, Miss Jacobs." With a wink, he started toward the barn, Pepper in tow.

She kept stride.

They tossed around a few lighthearted comments—nothing serious, and no mention of the events of the previous evening. Her mind flitted between how much his financial problems must be weighing on him, and the memory of their near-kiss the night before.

Just as they reached the hard-packed dirt near the barn doors, Adam faced her, rubbing a hand against the back of his neck. "Listen, last night, I—"

"I am *Angela Bijou*." The screechy declaration carried from inside the barn and sliced into the air between them. "I don't have to put up with this!"

Adam's face contorted as he and Courtney exchanged a glance. He loosely tied Pepper to the fence railing and held out a hand indicating that she should go first.

Courtney expelled a breath as she took the lead. If given the option, she would have handed over every last bottle of

Angela's precious *D'eau Douce* to know what he'd been about to say.

Angela faced away from the door, clenching and unclenching her diminutive fists, and stomping a tiny booted foot. She held her shoulders so high, her neck disappeared into the twisted chignon at the back of her head.

The collective attention of the room shifted to its entrance, and Angela spun around.

She fixed her fiery gaze on Courtney. "Call my agent, right now—" As her eyes shifted to Adam, her scowl melted to a sultry smile. "Well, hello." Relaxing her shoulders, she sidled over to him and, casting a deliberate burn at Jeffrey, draped an arm through Adam's.

Courtney retreated a step, her skin threatening to crawl right off her bones.

Lobbing Courtney a quick look, Adam covered Angela's hand with his. He considered the openmouthed crew, then spoke softly. "How about if we take a little walk."

Queasiness weakened Courtney to her core. Picking up her clipboard, she bit her quivering lip as the pair strolled past her and out into the yard.

A sound of utter disgust gurgling from Jeffrey's throat. "Now I've seen everything. Keith! This is the most outrageous display of ego I've ever—"

The horse in the stall behind him suddenly reared up with a thunderous neigh. Jeffrey lunged forward, sheer terror filling his eyes.

Keith bolted to his side. "Where's the wrangler? Why isn't he here?"

Clutching her clipboard, Courtney stumbled back. Several crew guys sheepishly glanced at one another. What was going on?

Mr. Kingsley attempted to calm down his star, who shouted out something about litigation. Just then, the wrangler swaggered into the barn and tried to grab the horse by its mane. He wobbled, winding up in a heap on the floor of the stall.

"That's it!" Mr. Kingsley bellowed. "I've had it with you showing up drunk. Get off my set!"

Drunk? Courtney gawked. Sure, the guys weren't exactly known for drinking Shirley Temples, but to imbibe on the clock was a well-known taboo.

The entire crew stood back, as if any sort of affiliation with this man might earn them their walking papers, too.

As the wrangler lurched and reeled off the set, slurring a blue streak and threatening to sue, Angela and Adam strolled in arm in arm. Courtney's breath caught in her chest at their obvious ease with each other.

Adam's attention darted to the agitated horse. He removed Angela's arm from his and hurried to the stall, instantly soothing the animal.

A still-shaken Jeffrey glanced from Angela to Adam, then back to Angela.

Angela scoffed. "What's the holdup? Don't we have a scene to shoot?"

"Yes!" Mr. Kingsley bellowed. "We also have an out-of-control horse, a cattle-drive scene next week and no animal wrangler."

Courtney spoke without thinking. "Why don't you hire Adam?"

Adam, who gently petted the muzzle of the movie horse, shot her an expression that screamed "certifiable."

"Perfect." Mr. Kingsley granted Courtney a look of approval. Marching toward the stall, he addressed Adam. "You'll start immediately."

Adam slowly shook his head. "Thanks for the offer, but no." With a parting pat to the horse's side, he turned to exit the barn.

Mr. Kingsley looked as if he'd been shot with a stun gun.

"What a brilliant negotiator." Angela's face lit up and she

crossed to Courtney. "Go out there and tell him I insist he take the job. Keith, the studio will just have to double whatever they were paying that lowlife drunkard. I want Adam."

Turning from Angela with an air of exasperation and defeat, Mr. Kingsley gave Courtney a *you'd-better-come-through-for-us-here* glower. "Tell him we'll lasso the moon if that's what it takes to get this movie made."

Courtney stood there, dumbfounded. Was this seriously happening? Adam needed money. And they were offering him the moon.

A vein in Mr. Kingsley's neck bulged an unusual shade of purple. He glared at her. "What are you waiting for? Go!"

Jolting into motion, she scurried out to the yard, where Adam now hoisted a bale of hay from the back of his truck.

"Adam, what are you doing?" She followed as he carried the hay to the side of the barn and dropped it. "This opportunity is too good to pass up."

He started back for the truck. "Look, I appreciate it, but there's no way I'd have the time to—"

"They're desperate." She scrambled to keep up. "Do you know what happens when movie people get desperate? Money starts flying like…" Her gaze lit on a bank of tall aspens rustling in the gentle afternoon breeze. "Like leaves in a windstorm."

"Courtney, they need a trainer." He grabbed another bale. "Which I am *not*."

"Oh. Right." Again, she followed him. "Pepper might beg to differ."

"That's not the same." He plunked down the hay near the barn and crossed to Pepper.

"Isn't it?" She stayed on his heels. "I saw how you calmed down that horse inside, and I know you can handle cattle. You said you needed a windfall, right?"

Unwrapping Pepper's rope, he tightened his jaw. "Yeah, but—"

"Do you have any idea how much a gig like this would pay?" She edged in next to him in the hope of getting him to stop moving and listen. "Name your price. Angela wants you to do it, and Mr. Kingsley is frantic. If you take this job, you could keep the ranch in your family. I don't know how much you need, but isn't it worth considering?"

He continued to untie the rope. "Look, I really appreciate the idea, but I have my hands full as it is."

"But God works in mysterious ways. You said so yourself."

"What?" Leading Pepper toward the corral, he looked away, distracted.

She stayed next to him. "Maybe you told me about your financial problem because God knew how this would play out. Maybe this is an answer to prayer."

"Courtney, you're making this really hard for me." His voice sounded weary.

She stepped closer and grabbed his arm, needing him to understand, not so much for her sake now, but for his own. He regarded her hand on his arm, then her face.

"Say yes, Adam. This is a God thing if ever I've seen one."

His lips parted as if he was about to speak.

A swoosh of fabric near the barn door pulled their focus off each other. Angela stood there, looking from Adam to Courtney. Her clear green eyes narrowed almost imperceptibly.

Courtney backed up, feeling her face flush. *Oh, boy.* This was not good.

Mr. Kingsley burst out of the barn with Jeffrey and several crew members at his heels. His wild gaze landed on Adam, and he hurried toward him. "There you are."

Angela took a look at Jeffrey and inched up to Adam. "If it's money that's the issue, just tell them what you want. They'll do whatever it takes to please the star." She splayed her fingers against her chest lest there be any confusion as to whom she was referring. "And having my cowboy around the set more will please me very much." She batted her eyes with a seductiveness that made the hairs on Courtney's neck stand on end.

Adam seemed unaffected. "I'm trying to explain that I already have a full-time job running this ranch."

"Keith, think about it." Jeffrey scrubbed a hand through his now-tousled hair. "There's got to be a hundred men around this place who know how to saddle a horse. They're a dime a dozen. He's nothing special."

Courtney's cheeks burned. Who did he think he was to insult Adam? This guy who was himself probably terrified of *kittens*.

She couldn't hold her tongue. "Then why doesn't the movie pay for a couple of those *guys* to take over Adam's responsibilities on the ranch for a few weeks? That would free him up to do the wrangling." She presented a conciliatory gaze to Angela. "And everyone would get what they want." She looked at Adam, who actually seemed to be considering her idea.

Jeffrey scoffed. "Keith—"

"That's a brilliant plan." Angela cupped her chin in her fingers. "But there's one more thing I need, Keith, or I'm walking off the picture."

A flash of extreme anxiety colored Mr. Kingsley's face. "What else?"

Angela took a few calculated steps toward Jeffrey. "I have to insist that the movie pay Adam a hefty fee to be the man who finally breaks Jeffrey Mark Caulfield of his fear of animals." Folding her slender arms, she stood in front of Jeffrey with a look of spite on her face. "He needs to learn to ride a horse."

"Ridiculous." Looking helpless, Jeffrey sputtered. "I—I'm not afraid...I just—"

"A hundred thousand dollars." Adam spoke with a quiet confidence.

Courtney's jaw dropped. Everyone stared in anticipation.

Adam looked directly at Mr. Kingsley. "That's what it

would take to make this worthwhile for me. You hire two hands and pay me a hundred K and I'll do it."

The color returned to Mr. Kingsley's face. He waved to his A.D. "We'll get it approved and contracted immediately." He hurried away, and the crowd around them dispersed.

Angela leaned in to Courtney so that only she could hear. "Arrange the dinner date now, Courtney, or that wrangler won't be the only one who's out on his ear today." Brushing past Adam, she seared him with an ardent gaze, then fired pure contempt at Jeffrey.

After receiving the bolt from the departing Angela, Jeffrey shot Adam a scorching arrow of his own, and followed Angela into the barn.

That left Courtney alone again with Adam. His back was to her, and she couldn't gauge his frame of mind. Cautiously, she edged toward him. "So, how do you feel?"

He raked his fingers through his hair, then faced her with an unreadable expression. She braced herself.

He scanned the horizon then looked her in the eye. "Grateful." A light smile coaxed his lips. "Thanks."

She closed her eyes as relief whooshed from her lungs.

The memory of Angela's threat tackled the lovely moment to the ground. Courtney started twice to speak, but stopped herself. Then a thought occurred. "Hey, remember that place you told me about—Esther's, I think you said it was called?"

His brow creased. "Right. Esther's Kitchen, up in Halston."

She nodded. "You said something about going there for a special occasion and you know," she choked past a knot forming in her throat. "It just occurred to me… What happened today is just that—cause for celebration. A really special occasion."

He looked as though he were trying not to smile. "You mean about the job you wrangled me into taking?"

Great. He was making a joke as he walked willingly into Angela's feminine web.

She fought back tears. Why was this upsetting her so much? She was stronger than that. "So. I was wondering if…" Her voice trailed off.

He held up a hand. "I know where you're going with this, and I'm not sure it's such a good idea."

"No?" Her stomach dropped. "But why…?"

Rubbing his jaw, he looked off as if there might be cue cards propped up against the mountains. "It's just that you all are only here for a few weeks." He met her eyes briefly, then glanced away again as though this was tough for him to say. "When the movie's done, you'll go back to your Hollywood lives, and where will that leave me?"

She didn't know if she should laugh or cry. He realized that the Angela thing was short term at best, and that wasn't what he wanted. He had character, after all. Of course, there was still her employment to consider. If he said no, she would be out of a job. She had to at least try for a save.

"I think you're reading this all wrong. I mean, it's really just dinner between friends. Nothing serious. Just a nice, casual evening. Can't we think of it that way?"

A slow air of contemplation came over him and he nodded. "You talked me into it. And you're right—this is cause for celebration. Name the day."

A dull ache formed in her temple. Why did this job have to be so hard?

Chapter 15

Adam sat at the best table at Esther's, tapping his heel nervously as Scotty McCreery sang about the trouble with girls. From this vantage point, he could see the purpling sky over the mountains while keeping watch for Courtney's arrival. She had said simply to be there by eight. Something about avoiding paparazzi. He had no idea there was salacious interest in the social lives of movie stars' assistants.

Leaning back, he gulped a mouthful of water. For the past week, he'd been so busy shooting the cattle-drive scene—far more complicated than any actual cattle drive he'd ever taken part in—and giving a couple of arduous riding lessons to a very reluctant Jeffrey, that he'd barely had time to think about this date. Now that they finally had a night off, he felt like a high school kid who had never even talked to a girl before.

"Hey, bro."

He snapped out of his thoughts as Janessa, clad in her white chef's jacket, slipped into the chair opposite him.

"Hey...." He checked out the window again for Courtney.

He was nervous enough without Janessa making him more self-conscious.

"No worries." She held up a hand in defense. "I'll get lost before your date gets here. I just wanted to tell you I set aside a couple of the cowboy rib eyes in case you guys want them. They're amazing and they're going fast."

Adam fidgeted. "Thanks. Now, if you don't mind—"

"Nervous, huh?"

He lifted a hand. "It's just dinner."

"Yeah." Janessa raised a brow. "It's not like Courtney's anything *special*."

He tilted her a look. "Courtney's great, but she's just a friend."

"Funny." She made that sisterly face—the one that said he didn't have her fooled. "You have plenty of friends, and I've never seen you bring any of them here. I must have been too busy in the kitchen to notice."

"You're hilarious." He tapped a spoon against the table. Who was he kidding? He wouldn't be having dinner with a woman if he honestly just wanted a friendship with her. And he certainly wouldn't be this anxious about it.

"It's about time you started thinking about your future." Janessa studied her nails, clearly not in any hurry to get lost. "I'm not going to be here much longer, you know. Then who will you have to rustle up your grub and listen to your problems?"

"I can rustle up my own grub, thank you. And Mama and Tandy aren't going anywhere."

"Adam." Her tone sharpened. "You can't convince me that you don't see yourself having a family of your own someday."

He yielded a look of surrender.

She leaned forward, keeping her tone confidential. "And you do understand that will involve forming a relationship with a woman?"

He shrugged and looked away. He'd always thought someday he'd have a wife and kids to help out around the place just like Dad had had him and Mama and Janessa. But Courtney? She wasn't quite what he had pictured.

Janessa leaned back and folded her hands in front of her. "Courtney's pretty perfect, if you ask me."

"She's terrific, but think about it, Ness." He lobbed back the challenge. "Can you really see her helping out in a cattle drive, or getting a calf unstuck from a barbed-wire fence?"

Janessa shrugged. "Why not? She took to riding a horse, didn't she?"

Gazing out at the foothills, he tried to come up with a retort, but all he could think about was how at ease Courtney had been on Pepper. Of course compared with Angela, who seemed as at home on a horse as *he* would feel in a limousine, anybody would have looked natural. Still, Courtney had an undeniable way with animals.

"She did great," he conceded. "But you know what life on the ranch is like."

"So she has to learn how to give medicine to a sick horse, or dig the truck out of the snow in the winter. So what?" She flicked on that sassy teasing tone. "She'd do it for *love*."

"Yeah, that's another thing. She's a California girl. She probably has no idea how harsh Montana winters can get."

"Adam." Her expression turned serious, just like Mama when she knew he had no argument. "You worry too much. Courtney likes you. Why else would she be coming to dinner?"

A feeling of nervous excitement churned in his gut. She was right. He should push all his negative thoughts aside and let this evening be about showing Courtney how grateful he was for her help in saving the ranch. God could handle the rest.

He allowed his demeanor to soften. "Thanks, Ness." He leaned in. "Now, get lost."

With a major roll of her eyes, she pushed back her chair.

As she stood, something outside caught her eye. Adam looked out to see the familiar Town Car round the drive at the front of the restaurant. He straightened. He hadn't expected Courtney to show up in Angela's car.

The driver pulled open the door to the backseat. Out slipped a woman with long red hair and huge sunglasses.

Janessa let out a gasp. "Angela Bijou!"

He scratched his chin, watching the woman tug at her almost indecently tight skirt. "That's *Angela?*"

Waiting in vain for the other door to open, he glanced at his watch. *A quarter past eight.* Where on earth was Courtney?

As Taylor Swift blared through the house's very expensive stereo system, Courtney danced from the laundry room, through the kitchen, and into the living room. She'd been at Angela's beck and call for so many days straight, this welcome night off gave her an exhilarating sense of independence.

Out of necessity, she wore the only clean thing she had left—the new little black dress she'd packed in anticipation of a cast party. Wishful thinking. Laundry day was the closest thing to a social event she and her new dress were likely to encounter in this town.

Just for fun, she'd styled her hair into a simple but chic updo and strapped on her black wedge-heeled sandals. It felt good to let loose, even though the image of Adam dining with Angela bogged down her mood like thick L.A. smog.

The sound of a car outside drew her eyes to the window and she stopped short. A red convertible skidded to a halt in the driveway, its driver barely taking time to shift gears before leaping out and bounding toward the house. *Jeffrey?*

Flushed, Courtney darted to the stereo and shut it off, then opened the door just as he charged up the front steps. Without giving her so much as a glance, he stormed inside.

"Where is she?"

"Angela?"

He looked around. "Who else? Where is she?"

"I…I don't…"

"She's with that *cowboy,* isn't she?"

"I don't think I should—"

"Listen…" He finally made eye contact. "Courtney, right?"

She nodded, surprised that he'd paid that much attention.

"It's really important that I talk to her *now.*" His voice actually quivered. "If she's out with him, I'm afraid she'll do something she might…*regret.*"

The emphasis he put on that word was like a fist to her solar plexus. She hadn't entertained the notion that something…*regrettable* might result from her successfully completing her job assignment.

Her thoughts snarled. "But, I don't—"

"I'm worried about her, Courtney." His focus burrowed into her. "Can I be frank?"

She looked away, uncertain of how she should respond. "Sure…"

He pulled in a supportive breath. "You probably noticed that she and I were dating a few weeks ago."

Tipping a nod, she wondered how much actual "dating" had been involved, but tried not to dwell on it.

"It ran its course like these things do, and I accepted that we were moving on. Then I noticed I just wasn't getting over her. I realized she means more to me than I thought, more than all the others. This is new for me—this wanting one particular woman."

Courtney shifted on her feet.

"Look…" His eyes glistened slightly. "I know I have a reputation for being Hollywood's Most Eligible Bachelor, but Angela's the kind of woman who could bring my bachelor days to a close."

Angela? Courtney failed to see Angela as that kind of

woman at all, but then she wasn't standing in Jeffrey's size twelve Stacy Adams.

"But now she's seeing that cowboy—"

"Adam."

He flashed a questioning look.

"His name's Adam." She gave her head a quick shake. "Go on."

"Yes. Anyway. It hit me like a bolt of lightning. I *love* Angela. I love her, and she doesn't know it. How could she know, when I haven't told her?"

Courtney's gaze shifted. Jeffrey loved Angela? That changed everything. What was she supposed to do now?

He ran a hand through his nearly perfect hair. "I have to let her know how I feel. Now. Before anything happens with that *cowboy*—"

"Adam."

"Right. So, see, I need you to tell me where they are."

She drew in a breath of protest.

"I swear, Courtney." He held up a hand in oath. "I'll never let on that you told me. Please."

What now? If she told Jeffrey where Angela had gone to meet Adam, she might lose her job. Even if Jeffrey didn't reveal his source—and how did she know she could trust him?—wouldn't Angela figure it out?

The thought of Adam sharing a meal with Angela pounded in her brain. Then the image of the two of them leaving together, going who-knows-where to do who-knows-what, made her heart nearly explode. And now that she knew about Jeffrey's feelings for Angela, it would be irresponsible of her not to stop this before something happened.

Throwing back her head, she blurted out, "Esther's Kitchen!"

His eyes enlarged and he bolted for the door like he'd been fired from a cannon.

Alarmed by his velocity, she followed. "Uh…Mr. Caul-field?"

His only answer was a low guttural grunt. Unless Court-ney was mistaken, his shoulders had actually broadened as he dove for the door. What was he planning to do?

As he burst out onto the porch, a man jumped from the nearby bushes, wildly clicking a camera in Jeffrey's face. With no hesitation, Jeffrey flung out a fist, sending the pa-parazzo's camera soaring into the bushes. The man let loose with a string of expletives as Jeffrey rushed to the driveway and leaped into his convertible with the same acrobatic dex-terity he'd used to get out of it.

Running after him, Courtney waved an arm in the vain hope of convincing him to continue a rational conversation.

The paparazzo frantically dug around in the shrubbery. "Aw, man. He's getting away. I have to be there when the sparks start to fly."

"Sparks?" Courtney went numb.

The photog was clearly frenetic. "He got wind of Angela's date with that ranch dude, and he looked like he was about to blow. When he gets like that, it's a sure sign that the money shot's coming. I gotta be there this time when he catches his woman with the other guy."

Cloudiness overtook her thinking. What had she done? "He gets jealous?"

"Jealous?" He snickered. "Man, I saw him nearly take the head off a guy he caught with that actress he was dat-ing last year. I think he put the guy in the hospital. Aha!" the man stood, camera in hand, and started to trudge out of the bushes. "Any idea where he's going? If I get the shot, I'll owe you dinner."

Ignoring his slight leer, Courtney started for a rusty Volks-wagen she saw parked down the drive. "I know exactly where he's going, and if you can get us there before him, I'll owe *you* dinner."

"Deal." Scurrying beside her, his pleased expression dropped. "Hold on, you're not going to warn off Angela, are you?"

"No." She yanked open the passenger's door. "In fact, I'll make sure you get an exclusive shot of her when she comes out of the restaurant."

Beaming, he hopped into the driver's seat.

"Esther's Kitchen in Halston." She buckled up, in anticipation of law-bending speed. "Do you have a GPS?"

"Are you kidding?" He fired up the engine. "In my line of work, it's only slightly less indispensable than the camera."

Chapter 16

Angela swept into the restaurant and looked around as if she owned the place.

Janessa scurried around the table. "I have to go tell the crew that Angela Bijou is here. Andra loves her. She'll flip!"

She darted back to the kitchen as Angela strutted in Adam's direction.

"Well, hello, cowboy."

She held out a hand as if expecting him to kiss it or something. Not quite knowing what to do, he gave it a firm shake and released it like an underweight trout.

Trying not to stare at that red wig, he weighed his words carefully. "Is Courtney on her way?"

Angela lowered her chin, a mini-volcanic eruption glinting in her pupils. She reached out and drew a long finger across Adam's hand, prompting a shiver of dread down his spine. "I gave her the night off."

He looked down at their hands, his apprehension intensifying. Subtly, he eased free of her touch and hooked his thumbs in his belt loops. "I know tonight's her night off. That was why we—"

As if on cue, Courtney bounded into the restaurant. She scanned the room, then darted toward their table. "Ms. Bijou..." She gave Adam a quavering half smile. "We have a bit of a situation. Could we talk outside?"

"Fine." Angela's jaw hardened. "But this had better not take long."

Courtney shot Adam a look of apology as Angela spun around like one of those high-fashion models, and the two women charged outside. Leaning toward the window, Adam could see them talking out front. What was going on, anyway?

Just then, a red sports car screeched into the parking lot and stopped next to the women. Jeffrey Mark Caulfield popped out like he'd been sprung from an ejector seat. Sensing that Courtney might need some backup, Adam headed for the door.

As he stepped out into the fading light, Jeffrey's voice carried.

"I can't believe you, Angela!"

"Are you insane?" Angela waved her arms. "Stop yelling my name for all the world to hear!"

Spotting Adam, Courtney grabbed his sleeve and pulled him toward the door. They both stopped as one of those crazy photographers jumped out of an old Volkswagen and started snapping away at Jeffrey and Angela. The pair hopped into the convertible and were gone in a flash with the photographer's car on their tail.

Adam rubbed his neck.

"I'm so sorry." Letting go of his arm, Courtney held up her hands in surrender.

"It's okay." Swallowing hard, he gestured toward the door. "Shall we?"

Her eyebrows shot up. Was she having second thoughts about their dinner? "I have to go. I mean—"

"Don't worry about Angela and Jeffrey. They'll be fine. Besides, isn't this your night *off?*"

She appeared to consider that. Suddenly, her expression brightened. "Sure. Let's go."

He held open the door, and she granted him a shy smile as she entered the restaurant. He heaved in a jagged breath. All this drama had sure rustled up his appetite.

Adam sat against the back of his truck cab, inhaling the mouthwatering smell of grilled onions that filled the night air. Nervousness volleyed with contentment as he glanced from Courtney to the crowded outdoor burger stand that had been his favorite hangout since his dad first took him and Janessa there as kids. After their fancy dinner at Esther's, bringing Courtney here for a casual dessert had felt just perfect.

She took a big slurp of her fresh huckleberry milkshake. "I can't get over how delicious this tastes."

"Best shakes in the county." Taking a sip from his straw, he stole another glimpse of her. Every time he did, her beauty struck him all over again. He loved that she'd dressed up for their date, but still looked like herself, not too made-up or anything. Nothing about this girl screamed *Hollywood*. She seemed like someone who was comfortable in her own skin, and to him that seemed way more attractive than all that phony glamour.

He nudged her elbow with his. "Maybe next time I can talk you into trying the buffalo burger."

"Oh, no way." She scrunched up her face. "Buffalo are way too cute."

Chuckling, he slanted her a look. "So I guess cows *aren't*."

"That's different." She drew the straw to her lips. "Some-how."

He leaned back, appreciating their easy banter. "Well, you seemed to enjoy that cute little steak you had for dinner."

"It was beyond delectable." Looking off at the moonlit mountains, she stretched her legs out and crossed them at the ankles. "I have to admit something."

His pulse skipped at her serious tone. He tried to sound relaxed. "What?"

"Well, remember those million or so restaurants I mentioned we have back home?"

"Yeah?" His mind eased a little.

She gave him a sheepish glance. "Esther's beats them all. Or all the ones I've been to, anyway."

"Oh, really?" A smile tugged at his lips. It pleased him that she'd liked the dinner, and he breathed relief that she hadn't pressed the conversation to a more intimate level. "Janessa sure likes working there."

"So she wants to be a chef?"

Swirling his straw, he finished the last remnants of his shake. "She's going to apply to some big culinary school in Seattle."

"Oh." She set her cup down next to her and drew the suede jacket he'd loaned her tighter around her shoulders. "So that explains it."

"Explains what?"

"Her burning desire to leave this paradise and move to the city."

Paradise? Did she really see Thornton Springs that way? Careful to keep a lid on his yearning, he stuck to the matter at hand. "That's part of the reason. She seems to have it in her head that city life is superior to small town life." He drilled her with a sarcastic look. "But I guess you could vouch for that."

Her eyes turned apologetic. "I'm sorry about the things I said. Now that I've been around for a little while…"

He leaned forward, trying to catch her gaze. "Yes…?"

She tossed him a sideways glance. "I can see the appeal. There might not be things going on all the time here, but maybe that's a plus."

His heart thumped like a herd of cattle. This was a very good step.

Her focus shifted to the night sky. "It seems like maybe Janessa doesn't appreciate how great she has it."

As encouraging as that was, it would be unfair of him not to be totally honest. "Well, I can't say as I blame her for wanting to try something different. Ranch life isn't like in the movies. It's a lot of hard work, most of it pretty dirty."

"Yeah?" Twisting her body slightly toward him, she tucked her feet under her. "So, what's your typical day like?"

He shrugged. "It depends on the time of year. During calving season, I'm pretty much gone 24/7. Catching what sleep I can in the barn or the truck in between helping out the birthing cows that run into trouble."

"Sounds intense."

"Plus we can't always save the ailing calves. That can be tough. Losing one means losing money."

"Oh…"

"Course, it's more than just the money." Where was he going with this? "Janessa gets pretty emotional when we lose a calf."

"I'd be the same way." Her voice had quieted. "I really love animals."

Was he nuts? It was like he was trying to sabotage whatever chance he had with this woman. He needed to lighten the subject before he blew it completely. "By the way, it looks like you were right."

"About what?"

"Well, I told Travis Bloom we had changed our minds about selling, but he's been to the house for dinner twice this week, anyway. Seems like he has some other reason for hanging around."

"I knew it." She pumped her fist in a victory gesture. "Mr. Bloom wants to date your mom."

"Guess so. And speaking of dating—" he cleared his throat "—I had a great time tonight."

"I did, too." Her nose crinkled. "Sorry again about the confusion earlier."

"It's okay. It was a little *strange,* but it doesn't matter now." He drew up his courage. "Would you like to, maybe, do this again some time?"

"You mean—" she made a sweeping motion across the back of the truck "—*this?*"

"Or something else. There are plenty of things to do around here on a date. We could—"

"A *date?*" Her head jerked toward him.

"Or *whatever* you want to call it." Nervousness spluttered out on a chuckle. "Only this time, *I'm* doing the asking."

Her mouth dropped open but no words came out. Had he just overstepped?

He held up a hand. "If you'd rather not—"

"I'd love to." With eyes as round as the brand on the cows at the Circle-O ranch, she chewed on her lower lip in a way he found undeniably endearing.

He leaned back. It was kind of a relief to think that maybe she was as confused about this as he was.

Chapter 17

The next morning, Courtney could have sworn her feet weren't even touching the ground as she stood on the bank of the creek that carved through the Bar-G.

She held a cup of tea for Angela as the hair lady fussed with her wig and they all waited for the crew to prepare for the day's shoot. A few yards away, Adam ran a calming hand down the long nose of the stunt horse he'd just attached to a wagon. Catching Courtney's eye, he lifted his mouth in a dimpled grin. Heat glazed her face. How was she supposed to concentrate on her work with him so near?

Ever since their talk the previous night, she'd been reviewing every conversation they'd had. There was only one possible conclusion. He had mistaken both her attempts at asking him out for Angela as requests for herself.

Embarrassment at her lack of clarity combined with utter elation. Now she knew that he had been pleased not at the prospect of dating Angela, but at the idea of spending time with *her*. That changed everything.

Did that mean he thought they had a chance of working something out between them?

Giddy and restless, she regarded her hectic surroundings. Jeffrey stood next to the fence he would pretend to fix in the scene, leaning on a shovel handle. From his far-off focus, Courtney couldn't tell if he had succeeded in his plan to profess his love to Angela, or how it had gone over.

"Ouch!" Angela screeched, batting at the hair lady's hands. "That's my head under there."

The woman's blank look gave the impression that she'd dealt with Angela's kind before and had long ago decided to internalize her response, letting her hairpins do the talking.

Angela grabbed at her hair and stomped away. "I could sue you for assault, you know."

Maintaining a safe distance between herself and Angela, Courtney allowed the soothing murmur of the creek to lull her away from the cinematic chaos all around. As she gazed across the expanse of grassland to the blue mountains beyond, she filled her lungs with clean morning air. Dropping her head back, she allowed the sun to caress her face in a way it never did when filtered through the L.A. haze. This must have been what they meant when they coined the phrase "heaven on earth."

"We're going again, people." The A.D.'s voice grated, as if to intentionally thwart the calming influence of nature.

Suddenly attentive, Courtney handed the tea to Angela, who took a quick sip before sloshing it over Courtney's hand and dashing to her place in the seat of the wagon. Courtney bit her lip rather than cry out in pain. Maybe she should take a lesson in detachment from the wig lady.

"Roll sound. Speed. Slate. Action."

Jeffrey sprang into character. "You hired me to fix your fencepost, Jessie, not your life." Following Keith's direction, he leaned on his shovel and tilted back his cowboy hat, his glycerin-sprayed face gleaming in the afternoon sun.

While the crew looked on, Angela called down from the wagon. "I can do anything that's needed around this ranch all on my own, Cord Hobson."

"Anything but fix a fence, it appears."

Angela made a playfully sour face at him, then clucked the reins as Adam had instructed. The horse hauled the wagon to the water's edge and halted.

"And cut!" Mr. Kingsley actually seemed pleased with the take. "I want to get this one more time before we shoot you crossing the creek."

"Reset!" The A.D. called.

Courtney held up a bottle of water along with the cup of tepid tea to Angela as Adam prepared to lead the horse back to his first position. As he took hold of the rein, he gave Courtney a wink.

An abrupt gasp drew Courtney's attention to Angela, whose eyes flitted from Courtney to Adam. Her jaw hardened.

Oh, no. The last thing Courtney needed was for Angela to suspect that there was anything going on between her and Adam.

"This time, Angela—" Mr. Kingsley appeared oblivious to the shift in his star's demeanor "—I want you to continue into the creek. The horse will stop in the middle, as we discussed."

"What?" Angela's tone sharpened. "Why wasn't I told about this?"

Mr. Kingsley looked alarmed. "Told about what?

Angela shot him a scowl. "That I would be required to cross that treacherous river."

"It's not a river…and it's in the script. Jessie's horse can't make it across the creek, and Cord has to rescue her. This location is exactly as it's described. I don't know how we could have—"

"I couldn't care less how it was described. No one told

me this would be a wet set." She fired a steely stare down at Courtney. "Why wasn't I told?"

Courtney drew in a sharp breath. *A wet set?* True, the creek was deep enough to meet the technical definition, but it wasn't like they were shooting *Waterworld*. She honestly didn't see the problem.

Mr. Kingsley flared a look in Courtney's direction as his face took on the color of a cranberry. "Yes, why wasn't this taken care of, *Ms. Jacobs?*"

The hushed crew stared. The only sound was the rushing of the creek, which gurgled along, blissfully oblivious to all the trouble it had caused.

Courtney faltered. "Uh…because I wasn't aware that—"

"It's your job to make yourself aware of your actress's needs even before she knows she has them." His voice escalated from raised to ear-piercing. "Haven't you ever done a film before?"

She could practically hear her spirit deflate under the weight of his words. "Y-yes, sir, I have." Turning to Angela, she spoke through a lump of emotion. "What do you need to make this right, Ms. Bijou?"

Angela huffed out apparent impatience with Courtney's lack of comprehension. "I'm supposed to be provided with a *dry suit.*"

The A.D. let out an almost inaudible moan.

Courtney bit her upper lip. "A dry suit?"

"To wear under my dress. I'll catch my death otherwise. I'm not continuing until you get me a dry suit."

She held a hand out to Adam, clearly expecting him to help her from the wagon. He eased her down and she brushed against him as she edged past. She cast a sideways glance at Jeffrey, who stood a little straighter and sharpened his eagle eye on Adam.

Angela's gaze returned to Adam, as well. "I'm so glad to see that *someone* around here knows how to do their job."

She tossed Courtney a disapproving glower. "Don't I look like I could use some tea?" Without waiting for a response, she hiked up her skirt and stomped off in the direction of her trailer.

Courtney's face burned. Everyone but Adam gave her a lingering look of disapproval edged with pity, and went about their business.

"Why are you still standing there?" Mr. Kingsley bellowed. "Get her what she wants!"

Courtney faltered. "I—I'm on it." With shaky hands, she braced the teacup and the water bottle against her arm and grabbed her cell phone from its pouch. Fighting back tears, she tried to punch in the wardrobe number.

"You okay?" Adam's voice was soft as he appeared next to her.

"Peachy." After a few pathetic attempts at dialing, she raised her hand as if considering pitching her phone into the water.

"Here, let me do that." Adam took the phone.

Calming slightly, she recited the number. A quick glance told her that he had tied the horse to a nearby tree and had come to her rescue when everyone else had walked away.

His hand brushed hers as he gave back the phone. A wave of electricity passed between them and, for a moment, nothing else mattered. Weakened, she realized she was falling head over heels for this guy, whether it made any sense or not. What a disaster.

A muffled *"Hello? Hello?"* reeled her back from the brink of her descent. Putting the phone to her ear, she started for crafts service, distracted—yet pleased—when Adam walked along beside her. She somehow managed to spit out the latest crisis to the wardrobe head, who sounded like she wanted to reach through the phone and strangle Courtney to spite Angela. The nerves in Courtney's shoulders twitched as she clicked off the call.

"Well?" Adam asked.

"She wasn't happy, but, she's sourcing a dry suit in Helena." Reaching the table, she set down the cup and bottle. "Not exactly a deep-sea-diving hot spot."

"True." He grabbed a paper cup and a packet of sugar. "But if I'm not mistaken, people wear them in lakes and rivers, too. She'll find what she needs."

She thumbed through the tea selection. "You're right. Sorry for my sarcasm." Grabbing an acai berry teabag, she tore at the wrapper. "I'm a little on edge right now."

"Understandable."

He dumped the sugar into his cup and was about to stick it under the spout of the coffee urn when Jeffrey stepped up to the table and fired him a goading glare. He reached for a cup of his own and quickly cut in to fill it with coffee.

Anxious to defuse any brewing tension, Courtney assumed a professional but sprightly air. "Good morning, Mr. Caulfield."

Carefully drawing the cup toward his lips, Jeffrey bobbed a greeting and mumbled something indiscernible.

Courtney and Adam shared a look.

She proceeded with care. "Did you have a nice evening?"

His brow wrinkled as he sipped the hot brew. Then recollection of their exchange from the previous night appeared to hit him. "Oh. Yes. Fine." With a parting nod, he started back for the set.

"I meant to ask you—" Adam paused as he watched Jeffrey move out of earshot "—what that was all about last night, anyway?"

Courtney raised her eyebrows, realizing now how confusing it must have been to have Angela show up when he had been expecting *her*. "Let's just say that he and Angela have some unresolved issues. Something tells me things didn't go his way last night."

Adam eyed Jeffrey with sympathy. "Angela's got him wrapped around her finger."

His light tone pleased her. Clearly, he wasn't interested in Angela and didn't see Jeffrey as a competitor.

Remembering the tea in her hand, she jolted. "Speaking of Angela, I'd better get this to her or she'll wrap her fingers around my *neck*."

Balancing the cup, she walked to Angela's trailer and tapped lightly on the door. Inside, Angela stood at the mirror touching up her blush. Courtney set the tea down in front of her and steadied her voice.

"Is there anything else you need, Ms. Bijou?"

"Yes." The word came out clipped and shrill. "I want you to arrange a dinner date for me with Adam at the house, and make sure Jeffrey knows about it—after the fact this time. That will drive him crazy."

Courtney stared at Angela as her motive suddenly became crystal clear. This whole thing was to make Jeffrey jealous at Adam's expense.

Her breathing became uneven, like she might hyperventilate. Even without knowing Adam's true feelings, she couldn't take part in this anymore. It was self-serving and downright cruel.

She steadied her voice. "Ms. Bijou, I don't think I can—"

"Do you like your job, Courtney?" Leaning closer to the mirror, Angela ran her index finger under her lashes.

"Well...yes. Very much."

"Good." She picked up a large brush and started dabbing at her cheeks as if she wanted to blot them off her face and start over. "Because if you'd like to keep it, just remember one thing. When Angela Bijou wants something, nobody stands in her way." She pierced Courtney's reflection in the mirror with a keen glare. "Nobody."

Alarmed, Courtney fumbled back. "I'm not sure I—"

"Just make the date, Courtney." Her words shot out like knives. "And make it soon."

What now? If Courtney didn't arrange the date, she would lose her job. That might not be so terrible, except that Angela had it in her power to have Courtney blacklisted, effectively cutting her career short before it had even gotten started.

Her thoughts tangled. There was no way she could allow Angela to continue to use Adam, or to break Jeffrey's heart. And how could she go on without Angela suspecting there was an attraction between her and Adam? What was she going to do?

Taking a deep breath, she closed her eyes. *Lord. I have to put this one in Your hands.*

Warmth filled her. She wasn't alone.

Chapter 18

The wait for filming to begin confirmed Adam's suspicion that he wasn't cut out for the movie business.

Leaning against the wagon, he wondered how long it would take the hair gal to finish messing with Angela's wig. Not that her hair was the only holdup. There was still no sign of the dry suit, and something was wrong with the lighting, *again*. He never would have guessed movie making could be so complicated.

His attention turned to Courtney, who stood a ways off balancing a cup and a water bottle, speaking into a walkie-talkie and taking notes on her ever-present clipboard. What a chaotic job she had.

He patted the horse's back, thankful that he was there to tend to the animals' needs and not some actor's. It disgusted him how everyone allowed Angela to use Courtney as her whipping boy. Even though he knew Courtney could take care of herself, he was glad he'd been there earlier to lend some support.

Joy filled him as he watched her brush a stray curl from her face. *Yep.* There was no denying it. In spite of his better judgment and best efforts, he was falling hard for Courtney. The question was what was he going to do about it?

When he'd checked his shooting schedule the previous night, it had hit him how little time was left. He couldn't let Courtney go back to L.A. without reaching an agreement with her. He wanted to think they stood a chance at something real, but without opening up that discussion he had no idea how she felt. They needed time to talk, and he'd have to grasp every opportunity.

"Ten more minutes, people," Mr. Kingsley's assistant shouted out, triggering a collective groan from the crew.

If he had ten minutes, he might as well use them wisely. He made sure the horse was securely tied off, then ambled toward Courtney. She looked up as he approached, then darted a quick glance at Angela.

He proceeded with casual restraint. "Everything okay?"

She nodded, securing the beverages between her clipboard and her stomach. "I just got word that the dry suit is almost here."

"Great." That wasn't exactly what he was asking, but he was glad for her sake.

Angling her head to see around him, she clipped the walkie-talkie to her waist and dropped all hint of attentiveness to their conversation.

He turned to see Angela clomping toward them, her mouth scrunched up so tight her lips had practically vanished. The wig woman followed, struggling to continue her work on the star's bobbing pate.

"The dry suit is nearly here, Ms. Bijou." Courtney's voice sounded strained.

"Whatever," Angela snipped. She fluttered a hand at Adam. "Did you ask him yet?"

Adam looked from Angela to Courtney. *Ask him what?*

Courtney seemed nervous as a cat, and her mouth moved with no sound. He was obviously missing something.

Angela puffed out air like a horse's snort. "Forget it. I'll ask him myself."

Courtney inhaled sharply and raised her almost-free hand in a stop signal.

"Well." Jeffrey sauntered up, using his prop shovel as a walking stick. He positioned himself between Courtney and Adam, opposite Angela—as if the four of them were about to commence square dancing. "Isn't *this* a happy little party."

Yanking against the wig gal's comb, Angela fired Jeffrey a glare. "And who said *you* were invited?"

As Jeffrey opened his mouth to respond, a woman with wild hair, and several tape measures tied around her neck charged up to Angela carrying a large box.

"Your dry suit, Ms. Bijou." The woman sounded pleased, and out of breath.

Peering into the box, Angela gawked. "Whose brilliant idea was *this?*"

The woman's face fell like an ax to a splitting stump. "Well...I was told...*yours*."

"Mine? Forget it." Angela pushed at the box, making the poor woman stumble back slightly. "I can't wear that. It's too bulky. You'll have to get something else."

She brushed the hair stylist's hands away from her head, and stomped off into the tall grass near the creek as if she'd reached her limit on human contact for the day. The woman with the box curled her lip at Courtney and trudged away.

Looking wounded, Jeffrey stared at Angela's back.

"Mr. Caulfield?" Courtney spoke softly, like you would to a feral horse. "Did you tell her yet?"

"No. I just—" Jeffrey worked his jaw "—didn't have time."

"Well—" Courtney tipped her head toward Angela "—you've got a few minutes right now."

His eyes flashed at Courtney and she gave a smile of encouragement.

Boosting himself up to his full height, he boldly strode toward Angela, clutching the shovel handle with both hands like a man who needed to go dig himself out of, or into, something serious.

Acutely aware of their dwindling downtime, Adam closed his eyes and shook off the previous exchange. He turned toward Courtney, hoping to draw her focus fully to him. "You had something you needed to ask me?"

"Oh. Right. I do." She heaved out a sigh. "Only it's not what Angela wants me to ask you."

Curiosity edged out his apprehension. "What is it?"

Seeing Mr. Kingsley coming their way, her face lost color. "Later. Right now I have to deal with the great dry suit impasse."

Assuming a businesslike air, she spoke up before Mr. Kingsley had a chance. "She's refusing to wear the dry suit."

He stopped short, as if her matter-of-factness had punctured a hole in his intended tirade. "Yes. I've heard." He lowered his voice to a near-normal tone. "And what are you going to do about it?"

Courtney shrugged. "I'm out of ideas. What do *you* think we should do?"

Mr. Kingsley's eyebrows flew up like a couple of spooked birds. He clamped his mouth shut, a first for him as far as Adam had witnessed. He appeared to search the dirt at their feet for the answer. "Well…I suppose we'll have to tell her we're shooting the scene as written and if she won't wear the suit we'll just use a double for those shots."

"Good." Courtney nodded. "Do you want to tell her, or should I?"

Mr. Kingsley graced her with a look of near admiration. "I'll do it, Ms. Jacobs. Thank you for your input."

They exchanged a restrained smile and Mr. Kingsley

headed toward Angela. Courtney looked at Adam, the corners of her mouth contorting in an astonished wince.

Adam couldn't help the grin that spread across his face. "Way to stand up for yourself, Miss Jacobs."

"Thanks." She readjusted all the items she still held in her arms. "I'm not exactly sure where that courage came from."

Just as he was about to respond, a piercing shriek turned both their heads. Angela flailed her arms as she screeched, eyes fixed on the ground in front of her. Mr. Kingsley and Jeffrey wavered back clumsily.

Without thinking, Adam dashed toward Angela, ripped the shovel from Jeffrey's hands and raised it like an ax. He aimed the blade at Angela's focal point in the tall grass and lunged, decapitating a large rattler just as it poised to strike.

Angela's screams dissolved into jittery moans as the entire crew quickly clustered in a half circle behind them. She threw herself against Jeffrey, whose round-eyed expression did nothing to conceal a frozen terror.

Mr. Kingsley took a few guarded steps forward. "Why didn't anybody tell me my set was crawling with snakes?"

Adam remained calm. "They don't normally get so close to people. This one must have been either deaf or injured."

Courtney appeared by Adam's side. "Adam, was that a…?"

"A prairie rattler."

"A *snake?*" She faltered back, her voice quivering. "Was anybody hurt?"

"Nobody but the snake," he uttered.

A couple of the crew guys kneeled down to get a closer look.

Adam raised his voice. "I wouldn't go near that head if I were you. It can still bite till rigor mortis sets in. Best to just leave it."

The guys jumped back, and the muttering crowd began to disperse.

Courtney continued to gawk in disbelief. "You just saved Angela's life."

He shrugged. "Even if she'd been bitten, we would have gotten help for her in time."

She shivered. "Yeah, but still…" Her eyes lingered on the poor dead creature. "A *snakebite*."

Adam sighed, grateful that he'd been there, and hating to think of how things could have gone if he hadn't been. Sure, a snakebite most likely wouldn't have been fatal, but it wouldn't have been pretty, either. And something told him Angela would have found a way to blame it all on Courtney.

Chapter 19

Courtney's head reeled, not just from the close call with the snake that morning, but from the rapidity with which Jody's PR team had spun it into usable promotional material for the movie. *Breaking Story,* the nation's hottest TV entertainment news show, had their star correspondent, Macy Kendall, on a plane bound for Helena even before the snake's rigor mortis had set in.

By some miracle—and promised trips to an exclusive spa once filming ended—both stars had managed to get it together for on-camera interviews. Although Angela had been too upset all day to continue filming, it was Jeffrey who'd practically gone into apoplexy. Courtney felt for him, coming face-to-face with his phobia like that.

All day Courtney had waited for Angela to revert from post-traumatic jitters back to normal diva ranting, but she had remained remarkably subdued. Now, as Courtney sat outside the trailer waiting for Angela to finish whatever she needed to do to make herself even more picture-perfect for the drive back to the house, she wondered when the other shoe would drop. It was almost as if the snake had scared the venom right out of her.

A cautious smile caught the corner of Courtney's mouth. This version of Angela was one that Courtney could possibly even grow to like.

The trailer door clicked open and Courtney leaped to her feet, fully expecting Angela to emerge with both guns blazing. Instead, she leaned against the doorjamb and furrowed her brow.

"Courtney, have you seen my teacup?"

Courtney twisted her fingers together. Was this a trick question? "Uh…no. Not since the interview."

"Right." Angela looked thoughtful. "Would you mind running back to the house to see if I left it there?"

She left it there? What? No irrational accusations?

Courtney set out, wondering if Angela's current reasonable behavior was actually some kind of ticking time bomb that would detonate once she'd had dinner and a good night's sleep.

Crunching across the gravel driveway, she watched for Adam, suspecting he had taken advantage of the afternoon off to get some ranch chores done. Even with the extra hands around to pick up the slack, she knew he felt a responsibility to do as much as he could himself. Too bad, since she wanted to spend time with him, and her days in Montana were officially numbered.

As she clambered up to the front porch, the door swung open and a couple of Macy's crew guys emerged, arms full of lighting equipment. They left the door open behind them, so Courtney entered without knocking.

Voices wafted from the parlor, and she quietly tiptoed to the doorway and peered in. Macy Kendall stood in the middle of the room with a man Courtney took to be her producer. With black reading glasses perched on her nose, Macy appeared slightly less dazzling than she had when Courtney had caught a glimpse of her before Angela's interview. Both Macy and the producer glanced up when Courtney appeared, then immediately returned their attention to their notes.

Unsure if she needed to explain her presence, Courtney cautioned a couple of steps into the room. "I'm just here to find Angela's teacup."

Macy pushed a strand of bottle-blond hair behind her ear and dipped a nod of consent.

Giving the room a hasty once-over, Courtney grimaced. Unfortunately, this was going to require a more thorough search.

"So we'll lead with Jeffrey's statement about Angela." Macy's tone seemed considerably more severe than when talent was present. "I really want to play up the love-triangle idea."

Courtney snapped to attention. *Love triangle?*

"It's a shame the rancher won't talk." Macy tapped a pencil against the notes. "I'll just have to put the meat on the bones of this story without any direct quotes from him." Huffing out a laugh, she shook her head. "Two hunks fighting over Angela. Now there's a ratings-grabber."

Courtney's face went cold. She had to say something. "Excuse me, Ms. Kendall?"

Macy regarded her from under an arched brow.

Courtney gulped. "You said something about Adam… the rancher?"

Macy's ears seemed to perk up beneath her carefully coifed bouffant. "Yes?"

"It's just that you… He…" Courtney stammered, reminding herself to keep a cool head. "I think you might have been misinformed."

Studying her for a moment, Macy flicked a hand at the producer. As the man went about his business, she removed her glasses and signaled toward the settee. Courtney perched, suddenly feeling like a celebrity in the hot seat about to be grilled.

Smoothing the skirt of her raspberry Anne Klein suit, Macy lowered herself onto the cushion. "What was your name, dear?"

"It's Courtney Jacobs." She made a quick search of her immediate surroundings, in case a microphone might be concealed in a bud vase.

"Believe me, Courtney." Macy's sympathetic manner seemed well rehearsed. "I would love to get the rancher's side of the story. It pains me to run items that are one-sided, especially when the person refusing the interview winds up looking bad."

Courtney's stomach did a flip that could have won it a spot on the Olympic gymnastics team. "I don't understand. He killed the snake. How could he wind up looking bad?"

Macy creased her brow. "I was puzzled initially as to why he would refuse my request for an interview. What hero doesn't want his day in the sun?" She looked pensive, her perfectly lined lips pursing ever so slightly. "Then Jeffrey told me what *really* happened."

Courtney's pulse skittered. "What do you mean?"

Macy pierced her with an unwavering, Maybelline-lined gaze. "Jeffrey had been about to kill the snake himself when Adam grabbed the shovel out of his hands."

"What?" Disbelief fogged her thinking. "But, Jeffrey was too scared to move."

"Well, most people *are* afraid of snakes—"

"No, this is different." Determination to protect Adam hijacked her mind. "He was frozen in fear because he has a major phobia of animals. *All* animals."

"Oh, really." Macy seemed to consider this.

"Besides, if Jeffrey were getting ready to kill the snake, why would Adam interfere?"

"Well, from what I gather—" a shrewd eyebrow extended

upward "—Adam did it as part of his plan to break up Jeffrey and Angela."

"That's not true!" Courtney lost her fight to keep a controlled tone.

"Oh, so you're saying that Jeffrey and Angela weren't together?"

"No. I mean…" Courtney huffed out exasperation, resolving to set the record straight for Adam's sake. "They dated for a few weeks, but they were at each other's throats the entire time. Then when Angela saw Adam, she totally went after him."

"Oh, I doubt that." Macy peered down her nose, making no attempt to conceal the disdain in her unnaturally azure eyes. "Have you seen the list of men she's been linked to? All of them superstar actors or mega-athletes. I can't see her going after a ranch hand."

"Ranch *owner*," Courtney corrected. "And she's been after him since we got here."

"Courtney—" Macy's eyes became skeptical slits "—I really doubt *you* would know."

"Of course I *know*." Courtney pounded her fists against her thighs. "I was right there in the middle of it. She had me set her up on a date with Adam. Two dates. For a diversion, she said. Then I realized it was all to make Jeffrey jealous."

"Oh?" That seemed to snag her attention.

"Adam never had any interest in her." Her blood boiled at the thought. "Do you know why? Because he has integrity. He wouldn't take advantage of a woman just because she's a beautiful movie star. He's not like that."

"I see." Macy drummed her fingers on her knee. "Well, whatever his motive, if he killed the snake, why not talk about it?"

"Because he's humble. He did what anybody would have done." She lifted one shoulder. "Well, anybody but *Jeffrey*. He wouldn't want to seem boastful."

Macy cocked her head. "I respect his desire to remain unassuming. That's so refreshing these days." She patted Courtney's hand. "Thank you, Courtney. You've filled in the gaps for me."

"I have?"

"Yes." Standing, she touched the tip of her glasses to her temple. "But without the love triangle, this snake story loses its bite."

Courtney shifted. Where was she going with this?

Macy paced in front of the settee. "The question is, how to find a fresh slant."

She abruptly stopped, with a snap of her fingers so loud it made Courtney jump.

"I've got it. I'm dropping the romance angle completely. I think the *real* story here is how this quaint town has rallied together around making the movie." Her gaze turned far off, as this new approach appeared to gather steam in her mind. "I can lead with the snake incident—just a quick mention of how a local hero rescued Angela Bijou." Her attention returned to Courtney. "That way, Adam will be given credit but without too much fanfare."

Courtney considered. This might be good.

Macy splayed her hands in front of her, palms forward. "Then I'll segue into a feature on the town. If I tell the people about this unspoiled gem, they'll flock here in droves to see where the movie was shot." Looking pleased with herself, she smiled decisively. "Courtney, you and I will put Thornton Springs on the map."

"Really?" Standing, Courtney beamed. This could be just the financial boost the town needed.

"Now, I have work to do." Shouldering a large croc-skin business tote, Macy thrust out her hand. "It was a pleasure, Courtney. And thank you again for your help."

Shaking Macy's hand, Courtney fairly vibrated with astonishment. She'd actually *helped* Macy Kendall.

Macy moved to the doorway, then turned. "Oh, and I think you'll find your teacup over there." Pointing a long, manicured finger to a table next to the window, she raised her other hand in a parting wave.

As Courtney retrieved the cup, something vaguely troubled her. What was it? She shrugged it off. The only thing that mattered was that she had squelched a potentially devastating rumor about Adam going after Angela. Instead, the town was going to get some national recognition that could seriously boost their tourism.

She stood a little taller. Things were definitely looking up.

Chapter 20

Trailing behind Angela, Courtney entered the community center. With fifteen minutes till *Breaking Story*'s airtime, the mini-gymnasium-sized area brimmed with movie people and townsfolk.

Angela paused to take in the scene. "Do we have a table?"

Courtney pointed to the far end of the room, near a large screen. She'd asked Jody to stick a Reserved sign on the front table, although Angela herself hadn't made the request. In fact, she'd been so undemanding for the past several days; it was getting downright eerie.

As they wended their way through the enthusiastic crowd, the spicy aroma of pepperoni made Courtney's mouth water. Long tables stacked with pizza boxes lined a windowed wall, where a throng of happy people filled their plates and grabbed sodas. Courtney's spirits lifted. This town knew how to throw a party.

She caught sight of several familiar faces, while keeping

an eye out for Adam. Things had been so hectic, she'd barely had time to talk to him lately.

Reaching their table, Angela lowered herself onto a chair and folded her hands in her lap. Courtney hesitated. It was almost easier when Angela barked out orders. At least then Courtney knew where she stood.

She pointed to the buffet. "Can I get you anything?"

Angela contorted her mouth in thought. "I'd love a salad." Her vague smile seemed almost apologetic. "And a diet soda."

Forcing a congenial face, Courtney set off for the food. It wasn't that anything seemed *wrong* with Angela, but maybe that was the problem. There had been so much wrong before that now "normal" felt like cause for concern.

As she stepped up to the food table and grabbed a couple of plates, she sensed someone moving into line behind her. She turned to see Jeffrey sizing up the spread. Her nerves seized. Ever since her conversation with Macy, a righteous outrage had brewed in her gut. Who was Jeffrey to lie about his intention to kill the snake just to make himself look heroic? Just as she drew up her courage to really let him have it, he glanced down at her and flashed an earnest grin.

"Good evening, Courtney."

She swallowed her planned outburst. This wasn't the same brash, larger-than-life figure she'd grown used to seeing on the set. Somehow his stature seemed to have shrunk to a surprisingly human scale. If she hadn't known his famous face, she could easily have taken him for just a regular—if unusually charismatic—guy.

"Surprised to see me here?" His conspiratorial tone made her feel like they were playing out that scene in *Five Nights in Madrid* where he and his glamorous costar thwarted the bombing of the king's palace using only a breadstick and an earring back.

"Should I be?" Truthfully, the sole surprise to her was that he thought enough of her to ask the question.

"I felt like I needed to make an appearance." His eyes lowered. "It was a little humiliating, what happened with the snake."

"It was?" Taken aback by his candor, she wanted to reassure him. "I don't think anybody could have done anything differently."

"Just between you and me—" he darted a glance over his shoulder, then leaned in "—I'm hoping this show tonight will help sway Angela's opinion of me."

Compassion filled the gap left by her draining outrage. He might have spent years taking a backward approach with women, but he seemed to genuinely care for Angela. Maybe Courtney shouldn't blame him for whatever he'd said to Macy about Adam. He'd probably acted out of his own insecurity.

She gave him a reassuring smile. "I'll be rooting for you."

"Thanks." He inclined his head toward the plate she'd heaped with lettuce and a splash of dressing. "Is that for Angela?"

"Yes. This and a diet soda."

"I'll take it to her." The glint in his eye was more shy schoolboy than well-known womanizer.

"She's down front." Courtney handed him the salad. "If she tries to shoo you away, tell her the table's reserved for both of you."

Gratitude blended with suave self-confidence as he braced two sodas in the crook of his arm and disappeared into the crowd.

Smiling to herself, Courtney grabbed a slice of sausage-and-green-pepper pizza and shifted away from the buffet. Maybe Jeffrey and Angela had a chance after all.

Her stomach grumbled. She perused the crowd and took a bite of pizza, still seeing no sign of her handsome cowboy.

"Ms. Jacobs, I was hoping I'd run into you."

The sound of Travis Bloom's robust voice from just behind her forced a hasty swallow. Her mind raced. Why would he hope to run into *her?* Unless it had something to do with her ruining his opportunity to buy the ranch. Why hadn't she minded her own business?

As she whirled around, her voice came out on a cough. "M-Mr. Bloom."

Looking concerned, he reached for a bottle of water and handed it to her. "Are you all right?"

"Oh—uh—yes, sir." Fearing she might totally humiliate herself with a misguided gulp, she calmed her cough with a cursory sip.

Seeming assured that she wouldn't need medical assistance, he continued. "You're shooting in town tomorrow, is that right?"

Still quavering, she nodded.

"As you know," he continued, looking not at all like a man who was fuming over a lost real estate deal. "I've been putting together 'The Travis Bloom Project,' and I wanted to…" He paused, giving the room a quick once-over, then leaned toward her. "I would like to talk to you about it. Can you break away for lunch?"

Her heart skipped at least one beat, maybe two. This wasn't about the ranch. He wanted to talk to her about working for him. "Yes. Absolutely." She fought back a scream. "We take lunch at noon."

"Good. I'll see you at the diner."

Stunned disbelief washed over her as he melded into the crowd. Attempting to do a mini-victory dance, she twirled around and smacked pizza-first into Adam's firm torso.

"Whoa!" Removing his hat, he stared down at the greasy triangular imprint on the front of his sky-blue cowboy shirt.

Her hot cheeks snuffed out all hope of playing it cool. "Oh! I'm really sorry."

"Hey." He lifted a wry smile. "I was hoping I'd run into you, but not quite so literally."

Setting her plate down on a nearby table, she grabbed a

stack of napkins. "I can be such a klutz." She started to dab at his shirt, then froze. What was she doing? It wasn't like this was a problem she needed to solve in her capacity as personal assistant. This was the guy who had occupied her thoughts day and night for the past several weeks. Why was she touching him as if she had a right to?

Looking as stunned as she felt, he placed his hand over hers, generating an invisible current that propelled her heart into her throat. She lifted her eyes to meet his and felt herself getting irretrievably lost.

All of a sudden the lights dimmed, prompting a cheer from the crowd and a scramble for seats. Jerked into motion, Adam reached for the last chair at the table next to them and signaled for her to sit, then stepped back in consideration of the people taking their seats behind her.

Sinking into the chair, her whole body tingled. What had just happened?

As she faced the screen, Adam's presence felt as if she were wrapped in an electric blanket cranked high. They had shared a definite moment. Did that mean he had the same hopes as her? Hopes for some sort of future together?

It was all she could do to concentrate on the sound bites from Angela's and Jeffrey's interviews as they flashed on the screen under the show's familiar theme music. The camera then zoomed in on Macy, flanked by the Vegas-style set. Behind her was a large split-screen image of the two *N2M* stars.

With a toss of her impeccably styled blond head, Macy flashed a whiter-than-white smile. "On tonight's edition of *Breaking Story*, we're traveling out West to discover what Angela Bijou, Jeffrey Mark Caulfield and a snake all have in common." Angling her face just so, she looked confidently into the camera. "It seems the three came face-to-face-to-face on the set of Keith Kingsley's new Western, *North to Montana*."

She crossed to a second screen, this one featuring a shot

of the main street of town, looking postcard perfect. A boisterous cheer erupted from the crowd, followed by an equally disruptive *shush*.

Courtney watched in fascination. How Macy managed to maneuver around that flashy set in stiletto heels, say all her lines fluidly, and end up on her mark with a casual hand in her pocket was worth marveling at.

"While shooting on location in the backwoods town of Thornton Springs, Montana…"

Courtney winced. *Backwoods?* Her eyes darted from side to side. Maybe no one else had caught that implication.

"…Angela Bijou and Jeffrey Mark Caulfield became kissing costars."

Courtney's jaw slackened. What happened to "dropping the romance angle completely"?

"After a few weeks at each other's throats, they ended their tumultuous relationship."

Oh no. Courtney had told her that in confidence. Hadn't she mentioned it was off the record? A cloud of panic threatened to turn torrential.

Macy raised a practiced brow. "But it's what happened next that will shock you."

Did she say *shock?*

Suddenly the weight of what Courtney had done hit her with hurricane force. Like a total idiot, she'd blurted out confidential information to a reporter, without even considering that she might repeat it. Her mind raced. What else had she said to her?

"The pair appeared to be following the standard on-again-off-again formula they've both made famous. But did Jeffrey hope to put an end to Angela's wild ways? He might have succeeded…" She took an annoyingly dramatic pause. "If it hadn't been for *this* man."

The screen changed to a long shot of Adam on Rocky's

back. A murmur ran through the crowd as all the blood drained from Courtney's face.

Macy continued. "Angela Bijou's personal assistant told me herself that the star instructed her to set her up with this gorgeous owner of the ranch where they're filming. All as a ploy to make Jeffrey jealous."

No! The room started to spin and Courtney had the sensation of floating outside her own body. This was worse than horrible.

Terrified of Adam's reaction, she stared straight ahead. She wanted to die. Not *die* exactly, but to at least fall into a convenient coma for a while. She didn't deserve to live.

The rest of the show was a blur of select snippets from the stars' interviews, supporting everything Courtney had told Macy. When she finally got around to reporting the snake incident, it was entirely focused on how Jeffrey, the death-defying hero of half a dozen action films, had frozen in terror due to his "zoophobia." Was that even a real word?

As the screen went black and the lights came up, the place became a flurry of movement and loudly expressed opinions. Courtney wanted to bury her face in her hands, but her arms had gone numb. Horror swelled in her chest. She was officially the stupidest woman on earth.

Slowly, she turned to face Adam. When their eyes met, his face hardened. He pushed off the wall with his shoulder and headed for the door.

Bounding to her feet, she moved to follow, but Jody unexpectedly blocked her path, as if she might want to practice a few kick-boxing moves on Courtney's skull.

"Do you realize how much damage control I have to do now, thanks to you?" Apparently not expecting an answer, Jody stormed off, raising her cell phone to her ear.

Confusion seized Courtney's mind as her eyes zipped around. She had to get to Adam but he had disappeared into the crowd. She pushed her way to the door and looked up and down the empty street. Her mind raced as she spotted him up the block, striding toward his truck.

"Adam!"

He flinched slightly but didn't slow.

Determined not to let him get away, she took off like a bank robber, grateful for her decision to wear her Sketchers tonight instead of the cowboy boots.

"Adam!" She closed the distance between them. "You have to let me explain."

"No need." Eyes fixed dead ahead, his shoulders tightened. "I understand completely."

"No. You don't." She trotted to keep up. "There's more to it, I swear."

"Sorry I couldn't be more accommodating about the whole date thing." He kept his tone steady and unemotional. "But you were a little unclear."

"Please—"

"And if you don't mind, I'd rather feel like a fool in *private*."

"But why would you feel like—"

"Because…" Reaching his truck, he yanked open the driver's side door. "I thought you were asking me out."

"I was." She slid between his door and the Jeep parked next to it.

"No." With one hand braced on the top of the door, he fired his words like arrows. "I thought you were asking me to go out with *you*. Not your boss." He slid onto the seat, his head moving from side to side. "I'm such an idiot."

"I'm sorry." She took a step closer to him, hoping to prevent him from shutting the door. "I didn't know."

Impatience edged his tone. "Didn't know *what?*"

"That you were the kind of person you are."

He fired a look that pierced her heart. "Oh, so if I had been a different kind of person, it would have been okay?"

"No." Confusion had her in its grip. "Please understand. I was just doing my job."

"Yeah, some job." He aimed his gaze at the dirt-spattered windshield. "Now I finally see what kind of person *you* are."

His words cut straight through her. "What do you mean?"

"I can't believe I didn't see it." A chuckle sputtered from his lips. "I actually helped you trick Angela with the water. Then we forged the autographs." He ran a hand over his eyes. "Why was I so blind? I knew those things were deceptive, but I wanted to help you."

Panic came in waves. "But it's not *me* who's deceptive. It's this business."

"Oh, right." His chin dipped in mock understanding. "And there's 'no place for God' in your business. Well, I don't think the *business* is the problem." His eyes blazed into her. "I think you haven't left any room for God in *you*." Twisting the key in the ignition, he brought the engine to life. "I have to go."

"Adam…I…" Her attempt to speak came out in short, gasping breaths as she realized he was right. Defeated, she faltered back till she pressed into the side of the Jeep.

His door slammed shut and she clutched her elbows and gulped for breath. Through tear-blurred eyes, she watched the truck rumble out of the parking space and pull away. Crumpling her face into her hands, she listened as the sound grew distant.

Just an hour before, she'd been on top of the world. Now, she'd be lucky if the town didn't run her out on a rail. The worst part was she probably had it coming.

Chapter 21

Adam steered his truck onto the pitch-black highway, trying to push all thoughts of Courtney out of his mind. What a fool he'd been, thinking she was actually interested in him when all along she'd just been facilitating Angela's scheme to take advantage of him. How could he not have seen it?

As the truck bumped along, he turned on the radio to drown out his thoughts. It didn't work. In his mind, he still saw her face. *Oh, man.* He really had it bad.

Concentrating on the curves in the road, he absentmindedly sang along with Matthew West. The lyrics came to him, without his even realizing he knew them.

"It takes everything you have just to say the word..."

He let out a long breath, knowing what was coming next. *Forgiveness.*

"Really, Lord?" He cast his gaze upward. "You're not even going to let me have an hour to wallow in this?"

He bit back the emotion he generally kept at bay except for his weakest moments, and then just when he was alone.

That was the only time he could admit how much he missed his dad.

Adam had thought more than once that he'd been cheated out of ten years of fatherly advice. Could be that was a part of the reason he had never gotten serious with any woman. There hadn't been a man to guide him through that part of his life.

He needed him now. If only Dad could be at the house when he got there. They could sit on the front porch and talk this thing through. But it hadn't worked out that way. That thought only served to intensify the anger he was already feeling.

Tightening his grip on the wheel, he focused on the road ahead and the sky full of stars. Emotions churned. He needed to get this said.

"See, the thing is—" he spoke out loud, as if Jesus were sitting right beside him "—I really thought I loved her. You know as well as me that I've never felt that way before. I don't think I'll be able to face her again before she leaves." His chest tightened. "Forgiveness is a mighty tall order."

Pulling onto the road up to the house, he drew in a long breath. God wanted him to forgive Courtney, but this was the same God who had allowed his dad to be taken away from him way too soon. Right now, any kind of forgiveness seemed about as far out of reach as those stars overhead.

Courtney leaned against the outside of Angela's trailer, which had been moved to the schoolyard for the day's filming in town. Having barely slept the previous night for fear of an angry mob showing up at her window carrying torches and buckets of tar, she couldn't remember ever feeling worse.

She checked her Swatch. Fifteen minutes till her now-dreaded meeting with Mr. Bloom. She had seriously considered just skipping it and sparing him the trouble of having to explain why he would never hire a turncoat like her, but that seemed unwise. She had to face the music sooner or later.

Not that derailing her career was the worst part of this whole mess, or even blowing it with Adam. The worst part was that she'd let God down. It had been ridiculous to think she could trick Him with some kind of Christian compromise. What did that even mean? Acting like a Christian when it was convenient for her? Adam was so right. She *had* pushed God out of her life.

The walkie-talkie on her belt crackled out a message telling the crew to break for lunch. She'd have to tell Angela she was going, but her stomach buckled at the thought. Angela had barely spoken a word to her all morning, and Courtney had a feeling that wasn't good.

She entered the trailer, where Angela sat at her makeup counter with her back to the door, her flimsy peach robe draped over her costumed form.

Courtney cleared her throat. "Ms. Bijou? I'm leaving for lunch now."

Angela fingered a hairbrush on the counter. "Is my sushi on its way?"

Courtney nodded. "With extra wasabi, just the way you like it."

Looking absently at the brush, Angela gave a tiny sniff. Courtney paused. Had she been crying?

Courtney wavered. It didn't feel right leaving her like this. With knees shaking, she inched forward. "I'm sorry for what happened."

Apart from a slight raise of her shoulders, Angela didn't respond.

Courtney gathered her nerve. "I realize now that I should have been more careful about what I said to Macy Kendall. It's just that she told me Adam was going to wind up looking bad in her story, and I needed to be sure that didn't happen."

Angela sniffed again, drawing her fingers across the brush like it was a tiny banjo.

"So I just wanted to apologize to you. I hope you'll forgive me."

When no response came, she turned and reached for the doorknob.

"So it's true then."

Courtney twisted a look over her shoulder. "What is?"

"You told that woman everything." There was an unnerving restraint to her voice. "About Jeffrey and me. And Adam."

Turning full around, Courtney hunted for a rationale. "I assumed I could trust her."

"Don't be naive." Snapping up the hairbrush, Angela shot a glance over her shoulder. "Everyone in Hollywood knows Macy Kendall can't be trusted."

Courtney sighed. *Sure.* Everyone knows *now.*

"So you just spilled it all." Angela's voice sounded clipped as she thumped the brush against the counter. "Without giving a moment's thought to how it might impact *me.*"

Courtney braced herself, torn between feeling encouraged at this glimpse of the old Angela, and worried that she was about to get the hairbrush flung at her face.

"You're right," she said quickly. "I just didn't want to see Adam get hurt. Or Jeffrey."

Angela glared at her own reflection. "And you didn't think about how awful everything you said would make me look?"

The muscles in Courtney's legs tightened, as if preparing her for a swift exit. "I know I had no right to say anything, but it was all *true.*" A prickle ran up her neck. "I…I guess I just figured you were impermeable."

Angela angled her head, her brows drawing together. "Meaning?"

"Meaning—" Courtney laced her fingers together in front of her "—it doesn't seem to matter to you what people think. You're Angela Bijou."

Whipping around in her chair, Angela draped an arm

across its back and speared Courtney with her trademark evil eye. "You think it's easy being me?"

The desire to choose flight over fight flooded Courtney's limbs, but her sense of duty held her riveted to the spot. "I'm sure not *always*."

Eyes still bolted to Courtney, Angela rose to her feet. "You have no idea what it's taken to get here."

She made a sweeping motion with the hairbrush, giving Courtney to assume she meant where she was in her life, not her actual physical location.

"Do you have any clue what it feels like to walk into a room full of actresses who look exactly like you, who are all up for the same degrading role in an insipid movie?" Her emotion rising, Angela began to pace. "To live with four other girls in a tiny apartment in the scariest part of L.A. because it's all you can afford?"

As that sank in, Courtney fidgeted. She had no idea Angela's life had ever been like that.

"And to have to flirt with a leering director because you need to make your one-fifth of the rent for the crummy apartment, and then to lose the part because you're 'not blonde enough'?"

Courtney's heart filled. That sounded pretty awful.

With mouth twitching and eyes reddening, Angela crossed the room and sank onto the sofa. "No. I'm guessing you never had to do anything like that." Her words sounded pinched as tears started to pool. "You probably went to college on your parents' dime and sailed straight into a career in movies on a wave of enthusiasm and your willingness to be treated like dirt by people like me."

Courtney wanted to respond but didn't know how, since what Angela had just said about her was largely accurate. Feeling awkward, she grabbed a box of tissues off the end table and perched next to Angela.

Dropping the brush in her lap, Angela took a tissue and

blew her nose. When she spoke again, her voice came out choked. "The thing is that the harder it got, the more determined I was to make it. It was all about getting what I wanted no matter who I had to knock down."

Courtney stayed completely still, afraid that if she said anything Angela might realize she'd confessed too much and would now have to kill her.

"Then when the snake almost bit me…" She paused as tears created rivulets down her thickly made-up cheeks. "It was like a voice from above telling me to take a look at my life. I realized I've been hurting people in order to get my way and not even caring." Hugging herself, she pulled in a gasp. "Now I have this big successful career, and lots of clothes, and two huge houses that I hardly ever see. All because I bully people into giving me what I want." She burst into sobs. "What kind of person does that?"

Assuming she didn't actually expect an answer, Courtney just gave a sympathetic nod and handed her another tissue.

Angela swabbed her mascara-run eyes and took in a jittery breath. "I was so upset about the snake, I just couldn't get it together to do any more filming that day." She turned to Courtney. "Do you know what Keith did? He *yelled* at me. He told me he's had enough of my behavior. Then he went and told Travis not to hire me." Her face scrunched up as a fresh wave of emotion hit. "I ruined my chance to work with my favorite director. That was my *dream*." Crumpling, she succumbed to a fit of howling sobs.

Courtney's shoulders stiffened. She wouldn't have guessed that working with Mr. Bloom had the same meaning for Angela as it did for her.

After a moment, Angela regained some composure. "Tell me the truth, Courtney." She looked up through puffy eyes. "Am I really that horrible?"

Discomfort cut short all chance of forming a coherent answer. What was she supposed to say?

"I need you to tell me." Angela pressed. "Nobody in my life is really honest with me."

"Well...I..." Courtney rolled in her lips. There was no way around it. This was her chance to speak the truth. "I wouldn't say that you're horrible. But I *have* had to do some things that I shouldn't have done just to keep you happy."

Angela's ruddy brow furrowed. "Like what?"

"Well..." She drew herself up. "Like filling your water bottles with spring water until the real *D'eau Douce* arrived."

"Oh?" She seemed puzzled. "You mean, I drank *spring* water?"

"You liked it better." Her courage rose. "And signing your name to those photos. That was wrong. Maybe even illegal."

"I see."

"But the worst thing was that I helped you take advantage of Adam. I never should have agreed to set him up like that."

"But..." Angela looked away, then back at Courtney, her eyes narrowing. "If you knew those things were wrong, why did you do them?"

Courtney scrunched her face. Wasn't it obvious? "Because I didn't want you to fire me."

Angela scoffed. "I wouldn't have fired you."

Creasing her forehead, Courtney stared. "But you said—"

"Don't you know I'm full of hot air? You're the best assistant I've ever had." She dabbed at her eyes. "If I fired you, who knows what I'd get? Most people won't put up with me the way you do."

A bewildered laugh escaped Courtney's throat. All this time, she had been worried about losing her job for nothing. That ought to teach her not to act out of fear.

Her tears subsiding, Angela stood and crossed to the window. "I really blew it on this movie." She looked at Courtney. "But do you know what the worst part is?"

Courtney hesitated. It actually got *worse?* "What?"

"Jeffrey." She gave a long blink. "I had my one shot at the real deal, and I messed that up big time." Staring outside, she rubbed her upper arms. "I got scared, and I did what I always do—I went after the next good-looking guy to make the old one jealous. I hurt people before they have a chance to hurt me." She spat out a sardonic snicker. "I'm a real gem, aren't I?"

Gulping, Courtney stood and crossed to her. "You know, I think Jeffrey would give you another chance."

"No way." Angela shook her head. "After the show last night, we had a huge fight. He said he doesn't want anything to do with me. He was so humiliated—not just because of Adam but for the way I let everyone know about that animal thing." Her face scrunched up again. "He said he can never trust me."

A dull ache throbbed at Courtney's temple. Regardless of how inappropriately Angela had behaved, Courtney had been the one to tell Macy about Jeffrey's fear. She was as much to blame for this as Angela.

She struggled for the right thing to say. "Is there anything I can do?"

A corner of Angela's mouth lifted. "Grab me a bottle of water?"

Relieved that Angela's crying seemed to be slacking off, Courtney went to the fridge and got an icy *D'eau Douce*. Just as she handed it to Angela, her cell phone bleeped a notification that she had a text. She jolted, suddenly remembering her appointment.

"Oh." Her eyes met Angela's. "I have to go. Are you all right?"

Angela waved a hand toward the door.

Stepping outside, Courtney checked her phone.

Jody. *Great.* Probably another lashing, only this time written out in text-ese.

Brace yrslf. M. K. is coming back 2 Thornton Springs 2morrow.

Macy was coming *back?*

This time, let ME do the tlkng

Fine, *let* Jody do the talking. Courtney started to speed walk across the school lot. If she had her way, she'd stay as far from the double-crossing Ms. Kendall as possible.

Chapter 22

Rounding the corner near the diner, Courtney slowed her pace and caught her breath. She was a couple of minutes late to meet Mr. Bloom, but why hurry to her own execution?

Through the window, she saw him sitting at a table with his back to the door, reading a book and looking more like a man of leisure than a movie mogul planning his next hit.

As the bell over the door signaled her arrival, the lunch crowd silently gaped at her. Who could blame them? She had wanted to help Macy put Thornton Springs on the map, and she had. The map of the "backwoods."

She steeled herself and headed for Mr. Bloom's table, unsure of what to expect.

Sheepishly, she slipped into the chair across from him. He glanced up, removed his glasses and closed his book.

Her jaw slackened. *A Bible?* Travis Bloom was a believer? *And* a huge somebody in Hollywood? If *he* could do it, maybe there was hope for her, too.

Fumbling for something meaningful to say, she uttered a feeble, "Sorry I'm late."

"Oh…" He consulted his plain but pricey-looking watch. "Well, what's ten minutes either way?"

She raised a brow. This guy didn't sound like any Hollywood director *she'd* ever known.

Joe approached and filled their coffee cups. "Afternoon, Miss Jacobs. Special today's that Reuben sandwich you movie folks like so well."

She drew in a breath. He seemed as friendly as ever, and she was pretty sure he wasn't the type to poison someone's food. She offered him a cautious smile. "Sounds great."

Mr. Bloom considered. "I'll have the same."

A modicum of relaxation eased through her as Joe went to put in their order.

"Now, let's get down to business." Sitting forward, Mr. Bloom assumed his professional persona. "Tell me about your experience working with Angela."

She drew back. This wasn't what she'd expected. "Ms. Bijou?"

"Yes. You see, I would love to cast her, but I've heard she's quite difficult to work with."

She gave a dumb nod, feeling totally blindsided.

"Keith has told me his opinion, but frankly he has very little patience with *anyone*. You've worked closely with her these past several months and I'd like to know what you think."

Relief that he wasn't admonishing her morphed into a nauseating mixture of despair and embarrassment. He hadn't asked her here for a job interview. This was totally about Angela.

Collecting herself, she carefully considered her response. "Ms. Bijou can be a challenge." Her shoulders drooped. If she had learned anything over the past few days, it was that she had to be honest. "The truth is, she's given me a pretty hard time. But I think she's done some soul searching recently. I know she really respects you and she wants this part. If you're upfront with her about keeping her diva antics in check, I think she'll give you a fabulous performance."

"I see." He seemed to let that sink in. "Thank you, Ms. Jacobs. I appreciate your candor, and I respect your opinion."

He did? "What about that show last night? I mean, I leaked personal information to a reporter. You still trust my judgment?"

Mirth played at the corners of his mouth. "Let me tell you a little something about this business we're in, Ms. Jacobs."

She held her breath. So he wasn't going to tell her she didn't have the right stuff for a career in Hollywood?

"At one time or another, every one of us has said something that's been made to sound far more scandalous than it actually was. I wouldn't worry about it. It will blow over."

Her brow pinched. "But…that show was supposed to make Thornton Springs out to be a great tourist destination."

He shrugged. "This town doesn't want to be a tourist destination. They want their ranchers to succeed."

"Oh. But—" her throat tightened "—that part about Adam…"

He lifted one shoulder. "As far as I can remember, nothing was said that cast him in a bad light."

She pondered. Maybe he was right. Still, she had lied, or at least she didn't blame Adam for seeing it that way. How was she supposed to continue to do this job if it meant treating people like that?

Her thoughts whirred and her eyes dropped to the Bible in the center of the table. "Can I ask you…?"

He inclined his head. "Yes?"

"How long have you been a believer?"

His face softened. "It happened three years ago, after my second divorce. I had managed to find huge success professionally, but total failure in my personal life. Even with all the money and fame I'd achieved, I had managed to hit rock bottom."

Talk about candor. Since he didn't appear self-conscious about it, she waited for him to go on.

"An actor in the movie I was directing heard a little about my situation, ironically from a segment on *Breaking Story*."

They shared a smile.

"He took me aside and asked if he could pray for me. Ordinarily, I would have thought that was a ridiculous waste of time, but he got me at the right moment. He planted the first seed."

"So, you don't feel like it's impossible? Living a Christian life and working in the movie business?"

He arched a brow. "On the contrary. We are needed there." He paged through his Bible. "Let me give you something to think about that has helped me through numerous trials." Finding what he wanted, he rotated the book to face her.

Her mood lightened. That verse had always been one of her favorites. *"'But seek first His kingdom and His righteousness, and all these things will be given to you as well.'*

"Seek God's will first in all things, Ms. Jacobs. Then everything will fall into its proper place."

She blew out a long breath. That was what she'd been doing wrong. Consulting herself first and God second, if at all. There could be no compromise if she wanted to live as a true Christian.

As Joe brought their sandwiches and they dug in, an unexpected contentment washed over her. Maybe she hadn't gotten the job she had wanted so badly, but she had gained something far more valuable.

Adam was right. She *had* come to Montana to find her lost faith.

Chapter 23

In spite of the tension in the air as the crew prepared to shoot the nighttime party scene, Courtney trusted that it all rested in God's hands.

She skirted the patio behind the ranch house as the set decorators put the final touches on the backyard. Hurricane lanterns adorned the twenty or so white-cloth-covered tables that dotted the grassy area, and dozens of smaller lamps illuminated the trees. By the time the sun set, the effect would be captivating.

At crafts service she made some tea, then started for Angela's trailer. As she dipped the teabag in the steaming cup, sadness washed over her. Since it was the final night of shooting, this would be the last time she'd see this big evening sky.

Hoping for a chance to say goodbye to Adam, she scanned the bustling area. Her heart ached. There were no animals needed for this scene and Adam hadn't signed up as an extra. She knew he'd given a riding lesson to Jeffrey today, his final duty for the movie. Now he was probably avoiding the place altogether.

Tears stung as she reached for the door to the trailer. When they finished up tomorrow, she would take off immediately for the airport. It looked more and more likely that she'd never see Adam again.

She entered just as the hair and makeup people were finishing up.

"Is this the best you can do?" Glaring at her reflection, Angela tugged at her fake hairline. "It's Jessie's big night. Shouldn't she have a little more…" She swirled her hands like the beaters of a mixer. *"Flare?"*

Looking bored, the hair woman packed up her tools. "You can flare up on your own time, Ms. Bijou. This isn't the MTV Awards."

Angela tugged a couple of tendrils free from her chignon. "You people are all against me." Catching Courtney's eye, she slipped her a subtle wink.

Courtney managed a small smile in response as the crew filtered out. "They're ready for you, Ms. Bijou."

"Fine." Angela stood, smoothed her skirt and headed for the door.

With a peculiar sense of relief that her boss's familiar fire seemed to have been rekindled, Courtney fell into stride behind her. They made their way across the drive to where *Breaking Story* had set up.

Courtney had been told they'd tape in the driveway near the barn, but Jody seemed to be waving them toward the corral.

"We're going in *there?*" Angela balked.

"I'm sorry about the last-minute change." Jody smiled through gritted teeth. "If you'll follow me, we have a pair of boots for you to wear in the mud."

After what looked like a moment of mentally cycling

through her possible objections, Angela shrugged and followed Jody.

Seeing Macy Kendall charging toward her, Courtney fought the urge to go hide under a hay bale. Instead, she firmed her stance and bit her lower lip.

"Courtney." Macy wore her signature form-fitting suit, paired with pink cowgirl boots instead of her usual stilettos. "I owe you an apology for failing to ask permission to site you as a source for my last report."

An apology? Seriously? Remembering Jody's warning, Courtney stuck with a curt nod.

Macy seemed oblivious to her restraint. "I had put together a wonderful feature on the town, but my producer is so one dimensional. He reminded me that viewers don't watch our show to make travel plans, but to catch the latest star casts."

Courtney couldn't keep her confusion from showing on her face.

"You know," Macy clarified. "Infotainment. Entertainment broadcasts." She let out a huff. "Oh, face it. They can call it whatever they want. It's still just gossip disguised as celebrity news. You have my apology. I get a little carried away, especially during sweeps."

Courtney gave up a conciliatory smile. She had to feel sorry for a woman who made her living spreading rumors.

As Macy and Angela took their positions with the barn and pink-streaked sky in the background, a crowd started to gather. It was no surprise that the local extras wanted to watch, but several crew members and even Mr. Kingsley joined them. Courtney craned her neck. Still no Adam.

Given her cue, Macy smiled and spoke into her hand mic. "Angela, I understand you've acquired a new skill for this movie."

"I've always wanted to learn to ride a horse. This was the perfect opportunity."

"It was even more perfect for your costar, and I'm told he has a surprise for us."

Macy turned, prompting Angela to do the same. A horseman in full Western costume galloped out from behind the barn on Miss Molly.

Courtney squinted. *Jeffrey?*

He brought the horse to a halt next to the women, and dismounted like he'd been doing it all his life.

Courtney's jaw dropped and, judging from the buzz around her, the crowd was equally stunned. A smattering of clapping grew to lively applause, prompting Jeffrey to turn to his audience and take a deep bow.

Angela looked more shocked than anyone as he milked the ovation. The second it began to wane, she spoke. "You are such a show-off."

Smirking smartly, he tipped his Stetson in her direction.

"Jeffrey Mark Caulfield." Macy radiated enthusiasm. "The last time we spoke, I reported on your fear of animals. You certainly don't look fearful now. What's your secret?"

Jeffrey leaned in. "I like to call it brilliant acting, Macy."

They shared a chuckle while Angela made a big show of rolling her eyes.

"The truth is—" he turned serious "—I do have an intense fear of animals. It's called 'zoophobia,' believe it or not."

Macy's head bobbed, as if this were new information to her.

"It started when I got attacked by a dog as a child. I've always managed to keep it hidden." He arched a glare at Angela. "Until recently."

"And what made you decide to open up about it now?"

"Two things, Macy. I was forced to learn to ride a horse for this movie. The man who taught me was the first person who ever said it was okay to be afraid." Jeffrey seemed to blink back surging emotion. "He then proceeded to make me *face* my fear."

A lump formed in Courtney's throat. Adam was such an amazing guy.

"You said there were two things," Macy said brightly. "What was the second?"

Courtney blinked back tears as Jeffrey disclosed how the previous segment on *Breaking Story* had prompted a slew of emails from fans who share his phobia. He insisted on coming back on the show because he wanted to help people. Who would have thought that of Jeffrey?

"One more thing," he continued. "The guy who taught me to face my fear of animals taught me to face something else, too. My fear of relationships."

Courtney straightened.

"Just today, he told me that you can't expect a woman to hang around long if you don't tell her how you feel."

Courtney froze. Adam had given that advice to Jeffrey *today*. Had he been thinking about her when he'd said it? A revival of hope sparked in her heart.

Turning to Angela, Jeffrey took her hands. "I love you, Angela. Please give me a second chance."

The crowd held its collective breath. Angela's eyes grew round and for a moment she looked like she might leap onto Molly's back and ride off into the sunset. Instead, she nodded, her face puckering as she gave in to tears.

A roar went up from the onlookers as Jeffrey wrapped her in an embrace.

Jabbing a finger in her ear, Macy shouted to the camera. "That was one love scene that wasn't in the script. This is Macy Kendall saying 'I love a happy ending'!"

As the TV crew began dismantling and the crowd started to disperse, panic coursed through Courtney's veins. She had to find Adam. If he had any feelings at all for her, she had to give him a chance to say so.

Her thoughts whirred. If he was at the ranch, where would he be? She glanced around. Jeffrey and Angela still stood in the corral, but it took a moment to register that Miss Molly was gone.

Then it hit her. *Jeffrey had ridden Miss Molly.* That meant that Adam would have to take care of her. This, not today's lesson, would be his final task for the movie.

Instantly, she knew where she'd find him. Darting through the shifting throng of technicians and extras, she made her way toward the barn. She heaved the door open and held her breath as she peered inside the dark, quiet space.

There he stood with his back to her, stripping Molly of her saddle. Her heart slammed against her rib cage. Sending up a prayer, she slipped inside, allowing the door to thump shut.

He twisted around, then stopped cold. An array of emotions passed across his face, and he moved to the saddle wall.

Frantic, she fumbled for words. "It was nice what you did for Jeffrey." Her voice sounded far away, as if it had come from someone else.

He grabbed a brush and returned to the stall.

Soldiering through a growing despair, she took a few steps forward. "It sounded like all he needed was a little encouragement."

His eyes fixed on Molly as he drew the brush across her neck.

The silence goaded her. She had apologized, and he couldn't even show her a little grace?

She folded her arms. If he was going to give her the silent treatment, he deserved a little honest perspective. "I remember something Janessa said one time. She said the two of you live to serve. Well, I do, too. In my job, I mean." She took a bold stride toward him. "But I made the mistake of taking my orders from the wrong people and ignoring the One who matters."

Adam worked his way to Molly's other side, turning his back on Courtney.

In spite of the pain that maneuver caused, she went on. "I

know what I did was wrong, but I told you I was sorry." A physical pull forced her to close the gap until all that stood between them was the gate to the stall. "I let the fear of losing my job cloud my judgment. Maybe you'll never forgive me, but I want you to know I learned something important." Anguish filled her. "You showed me how far I'd strayed from God. But I'm back now, ready to put Him first in my life."

He stopped brushing and raised his head.

Swallowing her trepidation, she rallied her courage. "I'm really sorry I had to lose my chance with you in order to gain *Him* back, but I can accept it if I have to. He always knows what's best for us."

Her heart ached. If Adam would just look at her, she would know there was hope, but he gave her nothing. It was no use. She had hurt him too deeply. Lowering her chin, she turned to go.

"It's just that I'm so angry."

The force of his voice yanked her back around. She stared at his muscular form, afraid of saying something that would render him mute again.

He spoke over his shoulder. "You made me think you were interested in me."

Her heart threatened to gallop right out of her. "But I was… *am!*" She gripped the top of the gate. "We had a terrible misunderstanding, but what you thought I meant, I really did mean, even though that wasn't what I was saying." Pinching her eyes shut, she shook away the illogic of it all. "You misunderstood my words but you understood my heart. So… please don't be mad."

His head moved deliberately from side to side. "That's not why I'm mad."

Her thoughts jumbled. "Then…why?"

Letting out a long breath, he stepped halfway around. "You are smart and funny and ambitious and you love the Lord."

Confusion washed over her. "And…that makes you *mad?*"

"No." Slowly, he turned, eyes cast downward. "See, God let my dad die. I was just a kid—fifteen—and He took away the most important man in my life."

A cold, helpless weight filled her soul. He was still hurting from that loss. That made sense.

"I never felt anything serious for any woman, maybe because I was in too much pain to let myself love anyone like that." He stared at the brush in his hand. "Then you came along, and this thing happened with Angela." Finally meeting her gaze, he moved to the gate opposite her. "I knew God wanted me to forgive you, but I realized I was carrying *un*forgiveness toward Him for letting my dad go too soon."

The moment stretched. She kept her focus on him, willing him to continue.

Closing his eyes, he spoke slowly. "So I finally forgave Him." He regarded her wistfully. "I forgive you, too."

She let out the breath she'd been holding.

He looked away again, tossing the brush onto a hay bale. "And now I'm madder than ever."

Her brow pinched. "But…why…?"

"Because I love you."

Her pulse thrummed against her eardrums so loudly she could barely hear herself think. He *loved* her? Everything in her wanted to scream, but she fought just to find her voice. "Well, if *you're* mad—" she leaned on the gate "—then *I* should be furious."

"Really?" His eyes filled with anticipation.

She nodded. "Because I love you, too."

In one perfect movement, he stepped around the gate and cupped her face in his hands. "Well now, that's a relief."

She giggled, emotion swelling in her chest. "So, *why* does this make us mad?"

Dropping his hands, his face turned solemn. "Because in a few hours you're going back to your life in the city, which I can never be a part of. This is my home." He spanned their surroundings with a wave of his hand. "Believe me, there's nothing I want more than to figure out a way to combine our two worlds, but I just can't see how."

Her joy faded as a cold heaviness settled inside her. He was right. It wasn't like either of them was prepared to take a chance on an entirely different life. He would hate L.A. She might as well ask him to move to Mars. And if she abandoned her career, she might wind up resenting him. That wouldn't be fair to either of them.

She stared through welling tears at the straw-strewn floor. If there was a way to make this work, only the Lord knew.

A rumble of voices brought her bleary-eyed gaze up and over her shoulder.

Mr. Bloom appeared at the door to the barn with Mrs. Greene on his arm. "We were hoping we'd find the two of you in here."

Seeming cheerfully oblivious to the sorrowfulness of the scene they'd walked in on, the older pair approached the stall.

Patting Mrs. Greene's hand, Mr. Bloom spoke to Adam and Courtney. "I have a piece of news that concerns both of you."

Looking down so he wouldn't see her blinking back tears, Courtney clutched her elbows. Whatever he had to say, she couldn't imagine it seeming very important right now.

"I bought the Circle-O ranch." Mr. Bloom radiated excitement. "Adam, we're going to be neighbors."

Adam reached around Courtney to shake his hand. "Congratulations."

"Thank you." His brow creased. "Now all I need is a personal assistant who understands the movie business and won't mind spending a good deal of time in Montana." He gave Courtney a wink. "Know anybody?"

Sputtering out an incredulous laugh, she resisted the urge to give Mr. Bloom a huge hug. Instead, she reached for Adam's hand and grinned. "I can get you my résumé ASAP."

Chapter 24

"Quiet, everyone!" Cal's voice crackled over the speakers, which had been strategically positioned around the backyard of the ranch house. "Time to introduce Mr. and Mrs. Adam Greene."

A wild burst of cheering and applause greeted Courtney and Adam as they stepped out into the golden June afternoon. She felt just like Angela Bijou exiting her limo for the *North to Montana* premiere the month before, except this was about a million times better.

She allowed her contented gaze to span the spacious yard, where their friends, families and most of the town had gathered to help them celebrate.

"You know…" She fingered Adam's black bolo tie, the one detail that had convinced him that wearing a tux wouldn't be entirely terrible. "This could get confusing."

"What could?" He placed a soft kiss on her temple.

"Your mom and I are both Mrs. Greene and we'll be living in the same house."

His focus turned far off. "I have a feeling that could change soon."

She quirked him an upward glance. "What, the name or the house?"

"Maybe both."

Her gaze followed his to the white-tent-covered dance floor where Travis Bloom lowered Adam's mother in a theatrical dip.

"Oh. I see." She chuckled. "She might be transformed into Mrs. Bloom, First Lady of the Circle-O."

"I wouldn't be too surprised."

Courtney smiled. She had grown to respect Mr. Bloom more and more over her first ten months as his assistant. His transitioning into the role of father-in-law wouldn't seem like much of a leap.

As she watched her brother Ben attempting the cowboy waltz with her best friend, Sheila, a whirring sound caught the periphery of her awareness. Searching the perfect clear blue sky, she saw nothing unusual. She leaned in toward Adam. "Do you hear that?"

He inclined his head, looking as perplexed as she felt. "What do you think it is?"

She shrugged as several of their guests stopped what they were doing and pointed to the sky above the house with hands shading their eyes. All of a sudden, a large helicopter roared into view directly above.

Playful accusation glinted in Adam's eyes. "Paparazzi?"

"Well—" she held back a laugh "—we're not exactly Angela and Jeffrey, but you never know."

As it became evident that the copter intended to land in the big pasture behind the barn, the majority of their guests began scampering over to greet it. Adam took Courtney's hand and they hurried to join them.

By the time they made it to the pasture, the copter had touched down and the engine had been cut. A man in a blue jumpsuit climbed out, carrying a clipboard and a large manila envelope.

He approached Adam and Courtney. "You the newly-weds?"

With an *isn't-it-obvious* glance at Courtney's Angela Bijou–gifted Vera Wang gown, the couple nodded.

The man held out the clipboard. "Sign here."

Adam obliged. The man exchanged the clipboard for the envelope and called some instructions to his crewmen as Adam tore at the flap. Pulling out a sheet of stationery, he announced to the onlookers, "It's from Angela and Jeffrey."

An excited murmur passed through the throng as Adam spoke softly to Courtney. "The note's from Jeffrey." He read. "'To commemorate your wedding, I want to free up some time for you two to dedicate to each other by paying the wages for an extra hand at your ranch.'" Wrapping an arm around Courtney's shoulder, he read on. "'This offer will be extended for as long as you want, since the gift you've given me—see the enclosed documentation—will last a lifetime.'"

Courtney reached into the envelope and took out an article from *Cinema Update* magazine. She read the headline. "'Jeffrey Mark Caulfield Takes on the Role of a Lifetime, Playing a Man who Rescues Elephants in Africa.'" Below was a photo of Jeffrey riding an elephant, looking the very epitome of an action hero.

"Well, I'll be." Adam went back to the letter. "'In gratitude to the people of your lovely *backwoods* town—'" he crooked a half smile "'—Angela and I have wired a sizable donation in your name to the town council, authorizing them to use it as they see fit. We hope this will provide Thornton Springs with a boost until we return to shoot *N2M2*—already in negotiations with Keith. And one more thing—'"

Their heads snapped up as a ramp clanked from the rear of the helicopter.

Adam returned to the page. "'Angela thought your guests

might get thirsty, hence the dramatic airmail delivery. Like the lady herself, her gift had to make an *entrance*.'"

Deciphering the words stamped across the sides of the crates that were now being rolled down the ramp, Courtney let out a horselaugh. "It's our own lifetime supply of *D'eau Douce*. We'll never be thirsty again."

Adam gave her shoulder a squeeze, then crossed to the men. "Excuse me. Could you open a few of those? He shouted out to their guests. "Everybody grab a bottle. We're drinking a toast."

A moment later, he walked back to Courtney with a couple of blue bottles in hand. Placing a palm on her waist, he caught her upturned gaze. She felt like the luckiest woman between Heaven and Tinseltown.

Glancing around to see that the water had been distributed, he raised his own bottle. "To my beautiful bride. God knew what He was doing when He sent her to Thornton Springs."

Emotion choked her words. "And to my handsome cowboy groom, who has promised to put up with me occasionally going Hollywood."

As the cool water trickled down her throat, her spirit soared. She had never imagined that their two worlds could blend so perfectly.

Firming his grip on her, he leaned down and gave her a lingering kiss that stole her breath. She pressed into his arms, practically oblivious to the catcalls from their party guests.

As they melted into a bear hug, Courtney thanked God for His wisdom and grace. She hadn't come to Thornton Springs searching for love, but the Lord had other plans.

Now, as she turned her attention to the deepest brown eyes she had ever seen, she couldn't wait to start their new life at the Bar-G Ranch—their happy home together.

* * * * *

REQUEST YOUR FREE BOOKS!

2 FREE CHRISTIAN NOVELS
PLUS 2
FREE
MYSTERY GIFTS

HEARTSONG
PRESENTS

YES! Please send me 2 Free Heartsong Presents novels and my 2 FREE mystery gifts (gifts are worth about $10). After receiving them, if I don't wish to receive any more books I can return the shipping statement marked "cancel." If I don't cancel, I will receive 4 brand-new novels every month and be billed just $4.24 per book in the U.S. and $5.24 per book in Canada. That's a savings of at least 20% off the cover price. It's quite a bargain! Shipping and handling is just 50¢ per book in the U.S. and 75¢ per book in Canada.* I understand that accepting the 2 free books and gifts places me under no obligation to buy anything. I can always return a shipment and cancel at any time. Even if I never buy another book, the two free books and gifts are mine to keep forever.

159/359 HDN FVYK

Name	(PLEASE PRINT)	
Address		Apt. #
City	State	Zip

Signature (if under 18, a parent or guardian must sign)

Mail to the **Harlequin® Reader Service:**
IN U.S.A.: P.O. Box 1867, Buffalo, NY 14240-1867

* Terms and prices subject to change without notice. Prices do not include applicable taxes. Sales tax applicable in N.Y. This offer is limited to one order per household. Not valid for current subscribers to Heartsong Presents books. All orders subject to credit approval. Credit or debit balances in a customer's account(s) may be offset by any other outstanding balance owed by or to the customer. Please allow 4 to 6 weeks for delivery. Offer available while quantities last. Offer valid only in the U.S.

Your Privacy—The Harlequin® Reader Service is committed to protecting your privacy. Our Privacy Policy is available online at www.ReaderService.com or upon request from the Harlequin Reader Service.
We make a portion of our mailing list available to reputable third parties that offer products we believe may interest you. If you prefer that we not exchange your name with third parties, or if you wish to clarify or modify your communication preferences, please visit us at www.ReaderService.com/consumerchoice or write to us at Harlequin Reader Service Preference Service, P.O. Box 9062, Buffalo, NY 14269. Include your complete name and address.

HSPDIR13R